The Sūtra of Golden Light

MLBD

SACRED BOOKS OF THE BUDDHISTS SERIES

Reprinted Under License from **Pali Text Society**

- **A Buddhist Manual of Psychological Ethics** : Translation of the First Book in Abhidhamma Piṭaka entitled Dhammasaṅgaṇī—With Introductory Essay and Notes by *C.A.F. Rhys Davids.*
- **The Book of the Gradual Sayings** : Translation of Anguttara Nikāya, the Fourth Collection of Sutta Piṭaka **(5 Vols.)**—Tr. by *F.L. Woodward* and *E.M. Hare.*
- **The Book of the Kindred Sayings** : Translation of Saṁyutta-Nikāya **(5 Vols.)**—Tr. ,Ed. & Introduction by *C.A.F. Rhys Davids,* Tr. by *F.L. Woodward.*
- **The Collection of the Middle Length Sayings** : Translation of Majjhima Nikāya, the Second Collection of the Sutta Piṭaka containing 152 suttas. **(3 Vols.)**—Tr. from the Pali by *I.B. Horner.*
- **Compendium of Philosophy** : Translation of Abhidhammattha-Saṅgaha)—With Tr., Introductory Essay and Notes by *Shwe Zan-Aung,* Rev. & Ed. by *C.A.F. Rhys Davids.*
- **Culavaṁśa** : Translation from German Translation by Wilhelm Geiger. A Continuation of *Great Chronicle of Ceylon* (Mahāvaṃśa) : **(2 Pts. in One)**—by *C. Mabel Rickmers.*
- **Dialogues of the Buddha** : Dīgha Nikāya, the First Collection of Sutta Piṭaka **(3 Vols.)**—Translation from the Pali by *T.W. Rhys Davids* and *C.A.F. Rhys Davids.*
- **Dictionary of Pali Proper Names (2 Vols.)**—*G.P. Malalasekera.*
- **English-Pali Dictionary** —*Venerable A.P. Buddhadata.*
- **The Expositor** : Translation of Atthaśālinī, Buddhaghoṣa's Commentary on Dhammasaṅgaṇī, the First Book of Abhidhamma Piṭaka—Tr. by *Pe Maung Tin,* Rev. & Ed. by *C.A.F. Rhys Davids.*
- **Conditional Relations [Paṭṭhāna] (2 Pts.)** Part I : Guide, Part II : Translation of Caṭṭasaṅgāyana Text of the Seventh Book of Abhidhamma Piṭaka—Tr. by *U. Narada Mula Patt Thana Sayadow,* Assisted by *U. Thein Nyun.*
- **The Jātaka or Stories of the Buddha's Former Births (6 Vols. in 3 Pts.)**: Translation from the Tenth Book of Khuddaka Nikāya of Sutta Piṭaka—Ed. by *E.B. Cowell,* Tr. by *Robert Chalmers, W.H.D. Rouse, H.T. Francis* and *R.A. Neil.*
- **Pali-English Dictionary**—*T.W. Rhys Davids* and *William Stede.*
- **Pali Metre** : A Contribution to the History of Indian Literature—*A.K. Warder.*
- **Points of Controversy** (Subjects of Discourse) : A Translation of the Kathāvathu from the Fifth Book of Abhidhamma Piṭaka—Tr. by *S.Z. Aung* and *C.A.F. Rhys Davids.*
- **The Sutra of Golden Light** : Translation of Suvarnabhasottamasūtra—*R.E. Emmerick.*

Pali Text Society
Sacred Books of the Buddhists, Vol. xxvii

THE SŪTRA OF GOLDEN LIGHT

A Translation of the *Suvarṇabhāsottamasūtra*

by
R.E. EMMERICK
Professor of Iranian Philosophy, University of Hamburg

MOTILAL BANARSIDASS PUBLISHERS
PRIVATE LIMITED • DELHI

First Indian Edition: Delhi, ***2016***
3rd Revised Edition: Wiltshire, 1996 (2001)
2nd Revised Edition, Wiltshire, 1990 (92)
First Published: Wiltshire (UK), 1970 (79)

ISBN: 978-81-208-4040-9

Also available at
MOTILAL BANARSIDASS
41 U.A. Bungalow Road, Jawahar Nagar, Delhi 110 007
8 Mahalaxmi Chamber, 22 Bhulabhai Desai Road, Mumbai 400 026
203 Royapettah High Road, Mylapore, Chennai 600 004
236, 9th Main III Block, Jayanagar, Bengaluru 560 011
8 Camac Street, Kolkata 700 017
Ashok Rajpath, Patna 800 004
Chowk, Varanasi 221 001

MLBD Cataloging-in-Publication Data
The Sūtra of Golden Light
Translated by R.E. EMMERICK
in *MLBD Sacred Books of the Buddhists Series*
ISBN : 978-81-208-4040-9
Includes Introduction, Bibliography, Translation, Index of proper names and appendix
I. Buddhism II. Suvarṇabhāsottamasūtra
III. Translation IV. Emmerick, R.E.

Published by

Motilal Banarsidass Publishers Private Limited
www.mlbd.com • mlbd@mlbd.com
Printed by Replika Press Pvt. Ltd.

CONTENTS

PREFACE

The present volume contains a literal translation of the Sanskrit text of the Suvarṇabhāsottama Sūtra. The original edition of 1970 represented the first attempt to render the Sanskrit text into a modern European language.

The translation is based on the elaborate critical edition of the Sanskrit text published by J. Nobel, Leipzig 1937 taking account of his subsequent improvements: the Nachtrag and Berichtigungen published with his edition, and various suggestions to be found in the critical apparatus to his 1944 edition of the Tibetan.

In the preface to the first edition I wrote: 'It is possible that it is because of Nobel's elaborate edition with its predominating critical apparatus that the Sanskrit text of the Suvarṇabhāsa has not previously been rendered into a modern European language. The words "verderbt", "dunkel", "unsicher" and the like are alarmingly frequent in his apparatus. Nevertheless, the textual corruptions have but rarely, if ever, obscured the meaning beyond discernment. Translation usually highlights textual difficulties, and I hope that by offering a translation I may succeed in attracting scholars to the task of solving them.'

The hope expressed has not remained unfulfilled. I am grateful to reviewers and others who have taken up the challenge presented by this interesting text and I have endeavoured to take account of their suggestions. Reviews that have come to my notice are: J.W. de Jong, *Indo-Iranian Journal*, XIV.1/2, 1972, 118-121; K.R. Norman, *Journal of the Royal Asiatic Society*, 1971, 197-198; F. Weller, *Orientalistische Literaturzeitung*, 1974, 387-393.

The Tibetan has been compared carefully throughout. In cases where the Sanskrit text is missing I have provided within brackets a literal rendering of the Tibetan translation, except in one instance where I have given a rendering of Dharmakṣema's translation because the fragmentary Khotanese shows that Dharmakṣema's translation may well reflect accurately the missing Sanskrit.

My original translation was intended to serve as a working tool for my own research on the fragments of Khotanese versions of the Suvarṇabhāsottama Sūtra. While working on the translation I was able to identify additional fragments and although I was aware that many more fragments remained to be discovered, I published as an appendix a preliminary list of those known at the time.

Although at the time of my original translation I compared the Khotanese versions wherever possible, it was clear as I mentioned in the original preface that they required further research and in many cases needed rereading in the light of my identifications.

When in 1975 P.O. Skjærvø visited me and asked whether I had any suggestions for a research subject suitable for a doctoral dissertation I at once proposed an edition of the Khotanese fragments of the Suvarṇabhāsottama Sūtra. After he had done much preliminary work by himself, beginning in 1977 we read the whole text carefully together. In 1983 his edition was accepted at the University of Mainz as Habilitationsschrift. Unfortunately the edition still remains unpublished.

It has accordingly been possible to make much more use of the Khotanese material in preparing this new edition of the translation. However, I have tried to restrict the apparatus to a minimum so as not to detract from the readability of the translation. Hence reference is made to the Khotanese only when it contributes to the interpretation of the Sanskrit.

Prof. P.O. Skjærvø is also preparing a new edition of the Sanskrit text of the Suvarṇabhāsottama Sūtra. It differs from that of Nobel mainly in the fact that he is able to make use of a Nepalese manuscript that was not available to Nobel. This is referred to here as MS. J. It is MS. No. 6 on p.163 of 'A descriptive catalogue of the Sanskrit manuscripts', *Memoirs of the Research Department of the Toyo Bunko (The Oriental Library)*, 37, 1979. I am most grateful to Prof. Skjærvø for making available to me a draft of this edition, which at present covers only those parts of the Sanskrit text for which corresponding Khotanese was known to him.

The more time I spend on the Suvarṇabhāsottama Sūtra, the more conscious I am that much work still needs to be done. Even now not all the Khotanese material has been fully evaluated although much new material has been published since the appearance of the previous edition of this translation: see R.E. Emmerick and Margarita I. Vorob'ëva-Desjatovskaja, *Saka Documents Text Volume III: the St. Petersburg collections* (= Corpus Inscriptionum Iranicarum, Part II, Vol. V, Texts III), London 1995 and my article 'On the St. Petersburg folios of the Khotanese Suvarṇabhāsottamasūtra', pp. 51-66 in: *Au carrefour des religions. Mélanges offerts à Philippe Gignoux* (= Res orientales VII), ed. R. Gyselen, Bures-sur-Yvette 1995.

The Sanskrit text as constituted by Nobel more than forty years ago clearly requires substantial revision. My original translation has evidently been helpful and encouraged further research. I shall be satisfied if this new edition, which alas has been made under great pressure of time and work, will similarly provide an impetus for continuing research.

The present edition does not differ substantially from the previous one although some corrections and additions have been incorporated. In order to reduce production costs this edition has been produced photographically from a printout made with the Hewlett Packard LaserJet Series IVMP using WordPerfect for Windows 6.1.

RONALD E. EMMERICK

INTRODUCTION

Any work concerning the Suvarṇabhāsottama Sūtra must owe a great deal to Johannes Nobel (1887-1960), who devoted much of his life* to its study. It is his edition of the Sanskrit text which is here translated. To Nobel also is due an edition of the main Tibetan versions and a translation of I-tsing's 義淨 *yi jing* Chinese version.

The considerable variation shown by the numerous versions of the Suvarṇabhāsa reflects its composite nature. Its compilation must have been largely completed by the begining of the fifth century AD when Dharmakṣema made his translation into Chinese, but the process of expansion and evolution of the work went on, and I-tsing's version some 300 years later is remarkably more extensive.

Nobel has demonstrated in detail in the introduction to his edition of the Sanskrit text that the Suvarṇabhāsa was built up around the Confession in chapter 3. Confession of sins, especially on the occasion of the *uposatha* celebrations, belongs to the earliest period of Buddhist practice. Birth-stories (*jātakas*) also belong to the oldest strata, and the Suvarṇabhāsa contains these too, the most famous being chapter 18 on the tigress†. A *jātaka* story provides the framework for expounding the important Buddhist doctrine known as the "chain of causation" (*pratītyasamutpāda*), which because of its greater philosophical value began at an early date to supplant the Four Noble Truths. The latter indeed find no mention in the Suvarṇabhāsa. Even the chain of causation, however, does not really exist according to the Mahāyānist doctrine of emptiness (*śūnyatā*), as is explained in chapter 5. Chapter 5 was clearly added to give the sūtra popular philosophical appeal by providing a brief explanation of the central tenet of Mahāyānist doctrine: not only does the individual not exist, but the elements into which he can be analysed do not exist either. In short, nothing exists.

* For his life see the obituary by W. Rau, *ZDMG*, 111, 1961, 6-12. A bibliography appears in *Jñānamuktāvalī*, ed. C. Vogel, New Delhi 1959 (= *Festschrift Nobel*).

† For a bibliography of this *jātaka* see É. Lamotte, *Le traité de la grande vertu de sagesse de Nāgārjuna*, Louvain 1949, i, 143 n.1, and M.J. Dresden, *The Jātakastava or "Praise of the Buddha's former births"*, Trans. Am. Phil. Soc., NS, XLV.5, 1955, 449 (no. 20).

The Suvarṇabhāsa was accounted in Nepal one of the nine Dharmas. Its importance to Mahāyāna Buddhists is revealed by the large number of translations and manuscripts which survive either wholly or partly. The Suvarṇabhāsa was translated not only into Tibetan and Chinese but also into such languages as Uighur, Mongol, Sogdian, Khotanese, and Hsi-hsia (Tangut). It was known in Japan already in the seventh century and played an important part in Japanese Buddhism.

It was the famous scholar and pilgrim I-tsing 義淨 *yi jing* (AD 635-713), who was largely responsible for popularising the Suvarṇabhāsa. Based on his translation are versions in Tibetan, Sogdian, Hsi-hsia, and Uighur. His translation seems to have owed its popularity to its clarity and elegant style. It completely eclipsed the earlier Chinese versions. The first of these was that by Dharmakṣema, who came to China in AD 414. His version was elaborated by the sixth-century translators, whose work is no longer extant. Paramārtha's translation and the joint version by Yaśogupta and Jñānagupta were among those used by Pao Kuei 寶貴 *bao gui*, who about AD 600 made a combined version out of the works of all his predecessors. I-tsing's translation, published in AD 703, is entirely new, although he too made use of previous work. Where he follows the Sanskrit he is closer than his predecessors, but he freely departed from the Sanskrit in the many instances where it appeared corrupt or difficult to understand. His version is therefore of little or no use in establishing the Sanskrit text from the one that survives.

There survive three main Tibetan versions. Tib. I corresponds exactly to our Sanskrit text. It is possible that this is the version made by Mūlaśoka and Jñānakumāra in the first half of the eighth century. Tib. II and III date from the reign of Ral-pa-can in the first half of the following century. Tib. II was made by Jinamitra, Śīlendrabodhi and Ye-śes-sde; Tib. III by Chos-grub. Tib. II follows a Sanskrit text not significantly different fron that used for Tib. I, but Tib. III is a translation of I-tsing's famous version. Some of the other Tibetan versions are based in part on a Sanskrit original as shown by C. Oetke.

In the opinion of Nobel, the surviving Sanskrit text cannot be dated earlier than the middle of the fifth century. Certainly Dharmakṣema seems to have used a more primitive version.

The only other versions of importance in establishing the Sanskrit text are the Khotanese versions, which, however, survive only in fragments. Their importance lies in the fact that they are close translations, made, with one important exception, directly from the Sanskrit. Considerably more of the Khotanese versions is now available than was known to Nobel and P.O. Skjærvø has investigated in detail their relationship to the various Sanskrit recensions and to one another. He concluded that the Old Khotanese manuscripts are based on recension B of the Sanskrit text, that is the original version reflected by the Sanskrit manuscripts A-G (and J) and Tib. I. He found no evidence for a Khotanese tradition based on recension A, which Nobel assumed to underly Dharmakṣema's translation and to be reflected by the Mironov fragments. As for the Late Khotanese material, some fragments appear to represent a primitive version of recension C, which Skjærvø considers to underly Pao Kuei's composite version and Tib. II. The Late Khotanese version contained in manuscript P 3513 follows I-tsing or Tib. III. Compare especially the conclusion (74v3-75v2 *KT* I.249) with I-tsing 413C, Nobel, Chinese, p. 94. Moreover, the Late Khotanese version of Sanskrit chapter 3 is described as *tcura'* 'fourth' (75v2) in agreement with the Chinese, whereas Sanskrit chapter 4 is described as *tcūram[ä]* 'fourth' (a2) in the Old Khotanese version.

It is to be noted that the title of the sūtra in the Khotanese versions is consistently written without *pra*. This is in agreement with the Central Asian Sanskrit manuscripts and renders it probable that Suvarṇabhāsottama was the original form of the name, although Suvarṇa*pra*bhāsottama occurs early elsewhere (Tib. I and Mahāvyutpatti 1339). The title applied originally only to the Confession in chapter 3 around which the sūtra was gradually constructed, as demonstrated in detail by Nobel.

In the translation bracketed bold numbers refer to the pages of Nobel's edition and bracketed superior numbers to the footnotes.

BIBLIOGRAPHY*

Bailey, H.W. — *Khotanese texts I-VII*, Cambridge 1945-1985 (vols 1-3 reprinted in one volume as 'second edition', Cambridge 1969 and 1980; vol. 4 reprinted Cambridge 1979; vol. 5 reprinted Cambridge 1980). (Abbreviated *KT* 1-7).

Emmerick, R.E. — *A guide to the literature of Khotan* (= Studia Philologica Buddhica, Occasional Paper Series III), Tokyo 1979; 2nd ed. Tokyo 1992.

Leumann, E. — *Buddhistische Literatur, nordarisch und deutsch, 1. Teil: Nebenstücke.* Abhandlungen für die Kunde des Morgenlandes XV.2, Leipzig 1920, reprinted Nendeln, Liechtenstein 1966. (Abbreviated: N).

Nobel, J. — *Suvarṇabhāsottamasūtra, Das Goldglanz-Sūtra, ein Sanskrittext des Mahāyāna-Buddhismus,* Leipzig 1937.

Nobel, J. — *Suvarṇaprabhāsottamasūtra, Das Goldglanz-Sūtra, ein Sanskrittext des Mahāyāna-Buddhismus. Die tibetischen Übersetzungen mit einem Wörterbuch.* i. *Die tibetischen Übersetzungen*, Leiden-Stuttgart 1944. (Abbreviated: Nobel, *Tib.*) ii. *Wörterbuch Tibetisch-Deutsch-Sanskrit*, Leiden 1950.

Nobel, J. — *Ein alter medizinischer Sanskrit-Text und seine Deutung*, Supplement to the Journal of the American Oriental Society, 11, 1951.

* For a fairly comprehensive bibliography see Nobel, Chinese, pp. lviiiff.

Nobel, J. — 'Das Zauberbad der Göttin Sarasvatī', pp.123-139 in: *Beiträge zur indischen Philologie und Altertumskunde, Walther Schubring zum 70. Geburtstag dargebracht von der deutschen Indologie*, (= Alt- und Neu-Indische Studien 7), Hamburg 1951.

Nobel, J. — *Suvarṇaprabhāsottamasūtra, Das Goldglanz-Sūtra, ein Sanskrittext des Mahāyāna-Buddhismus. I-tsing's chinesische Version und ihre Übersetzung.* i. *I-tsing's chinesische Version,* Leiden 1958. (Abbreviated: Nobel, Chinese.) ii. *Die tibetische Übersetzung,* Leiden 1958.

Oetke, Claus — *Die aus dem Chinesischen übersetzten tibetischen Versionen des Suvarṇaprabhāsasūtra, Philologische und linguistische Beiträge zur klassifizierenden Charakterisierung übersetzter Texte,* (= Alt- und Neu-Indische Studien 18), Wiesbaden 1977.

Simonsson, N. — *Indo-tibetische Studien, Die Methoden der tibetischen Übersetzer, untersucht im Hinblick auf die Bedeutung ihrer Übersetzungen für die Sanskritphilologie*, Uppsala 1957.

Tsuchida, R. — 'Textkritische Noten zum Sanskrittext des Goldglanz-Sūtra', pp.111-152 in: *Central Asiatic Journal*, 29.1/2, 1985. (Abbreviated *CAJ*).

TRANSLATION

(1) 1. INTRODUCTORY CHAPTER

Oṃ. Homage to all the glorious Buddhas and Bodhisattvas.

(Oṃ. Homage to the glorious, blessed, noble Perfection of Wisdom (Prajñāpāramitā), likewise to victory over the states of existence (taught by) divine and human tradition. Hail!)[1]

I heard at one time (how) the Tathāgata on Mount Gṛdhrakūṭa dwelled in the sphere of religion in the profound Buddha-region, (together with the noble goddess Bodhisattvasamuccayā, and with the great goddess Sarasvatī, and with the great goddess Śrī, and with the great earth-goddess Dṛḍhā, and with the great goddess Hārītī, with such great deities at the head (and also) with numerous gods, Nāgas, Yakṣas, Rākṣasas, Gandharvas, Asuras, Garuḍas, Kiṃnaras, Mahoragas, men and non-men.

Then the venerable Ānanda spoke thus to the Lord: "Lord, what will be for them the Discipline of the Law?" The Lord replied: "The essence of meditation and the Law is pure, established according to its manifestation and not by arduous inquiry.")[2]

Among purified, pure, best Bodhisattvas (2) *I will preach[3] the excellent Suvarṇabhāsa, king of sūtras, very profound on hearing and profound on examination. It has been blessed by the Buddhas in the four directions, by Akṣobhyarāja in the east, in the south by Ratnaketu, in the west by Amitābha, in the north by Dundubhisvara. I will proclaim this blessing, the excellent, auspicious confession, whose aim is the ruin of all evils, producing the destruction of all evils, conferring every blessing, ruining every misfortune, the basis of omniscience, thoroughly adorned with every splendour. For those beings whose senses are defective, whose life is expended or failing, beset by

[1] 'Oṃ ... Hail!' not in Tib. I and recognized by Nobel as a late insertion.

[2] 'together ... inquiry': late insertion according to Nobel.

[3] The Tibetan *hchad-do* indicates a form of *diś*.

misfortune, their faces averted from the gods, hated by dear, beloved people, oppressed in such places as households, or at variance with one another, tormented by the destruction of their property, (**3**) both in grief and trouble, and in poverty, likewise in the plight of fear, in the affliction of planet or asterism, in the violent grip of demons, one (who) sees an evil dream full of grief and trouble should listen to (this) excellent sūtra, when he has bathed well and is pure. For those who hear this sūtra, the profound Buddha-region, with pure minds and good intentions, adorned with clean garments, and for all beings such most severe misfortunes are forever extinguished by the splendour of this sūtra for the world-protectors themselves together with their ministers and army chiefs will provide protection for them with countless millions of Yakṣas. The great goddess Sarasvatī, likewise (the goddess) who dwells in the (river) Nairañjanā, Hārītī, the mother of Bhūtas, and the Earth-goddess Dṛḍhā, the Brahma-kings and the Thirty-three kings, the powerful rulers of the serpents, the kings of the Kiṃnaras and the kings of the Asuras, likewise the kings of the Garuḍas, (**4**) these, having approached there with the might of their armies and with their vehicles, will provide protection for them, by day and by night, unwearying[(4)]. I will make known this sūtra, the profound Buddha-region, the marvellous mystery of all the Buddhas, for millions of aeons. Those who hear this sūtra and who cause others to hear it, whoever rejoice in it, and those who do honour to it, will be honoured throughout numerous millions of aeons by gods, serpents and men, by Kiṃnaras, Asuras and Yakṣas. The heap of merit arising from them is endless, incalculable, inconceivable, for those beings who have performed merits. They will be gladly accepted by the Buddhas in the ten directions and likewise by the Bodhisattvas, whose career is profound. Having put on clean robes, wearing well-perfumed clothes, having produced a mind (full) of love, one must do honour untiringly. One should make one's mind, self, pure (and) expansive. (**5**) Purify (your) thoughts and hear (this) excellent sūtra. Those who hear this sūtra, welcome among men and a well-gained fruit of human existence, will live a good life. Those into whose ear this instruction enters will have their merit-roots ripened and be praised by numerous

[(4)] Read *atandritāḥ* for *samāhitāḥ* with Nobel, *Tib.* p.5 n.52.

Buddhas.

So (ends) the first chapter, the Introductory Chapter, in the excellent Suvarṇabhāsa, king of sūtras. (6)

2. Chapter on the Measure of Life of the Tathāgata

Moreover, at the time, at that period, in the great city of Rājagṛha there dwelled the Bodhisattva called Ruciraketu, a great being, who had rendered service to a previous Buddha, who had planted merit-roots, and who was revered by many hundreds of thousands of millions of Buddhas. Thus it occurred to him: "What is the cause, what is the reason, why the Lord Śākyamuni had such a short measure of life as eighty years?"

Then it occurred thus to him: "It has indeed been said by the Lord: 'There are two causes, two reasons for long life. What are the two? Refraining from killing living beings and giving away food.' Now for many incalculable hundreds of thousands of millions of aeons the Lord Śākyamuni refrained from killing living beings. He not only adhered to the course of action consisting in the ten merit-roots but he also gave up to beings food, and internal and external objects, until finally hungry beings were satisfied by the flesh, (7) blood, bones and marrow of his own body, how much more by other food."

Now while this good man was thinking this and similar thoughts of mindfulness and concentration on the Buddha, his house became vast (and) extensive, made of beryl, adorned with numerous divine jewels, a transformation due to the Tathāgata[(5)], filled with perfumes surpassing those of the gods. And in that house in the four directions there appeared four seats made of divine jewels. And on those seats mats made of divine jewels and fine cotton cloth appeared spread out. And on those mats appeared divine lotuses adorned with numerous jewels,

[(5)] The Sanskrit text has *tathāgatavigraha*, which is rendered in Tibetan as *de-bźin-gśegs-pas kha-dog bsgyur-ba* 'having its colour transformed by the Tathāgata'. In his *Wörterbuch* p.14 Nobel has under *kha-dog bsgyur-ba* 'das Farbe-ändern, vigraha (schwierig)'. Since Sanskrit *vigraha* can mean 'form, shape' and 'ornamentation' (Monier-Williams) the Tibetan translation appears to be in close agreement. In the Khotanese version however the counterpart of *tathāgatavigraha* is *balysavīya* and *balysu āṣaṇa*, both meaning 'worthy of the Buddha'.

transformations due to the Tathāgata. And on those lotuses there appeared four Lord Buddhas. In the east appeared the Tathāgata Akṣobhya. (**8**) In the south appeared the Tathāgata Ratnaketu. In the west appeared the Tathāgata Amitāyus. In the north appeared the Tathāgata Dundubhisvara. And those Lord Buddhas appeared immediately upon lion-thrones.

Then not only the great city of Rājagṛha was filled with a great light but also the triple-thousand great-thousand world-sphere and world-spheres equal to the grains of sand in the Ganges river in all ten directions became filled with light. And divine flowers rained down. And divine musical instruments resounded. And all the beings in this triple-thousand great-thousand world-sphere by the Buddha's power became possessed of divine happiness. Beings whose senses were incomplete became possessed of all their senses. And beings blind from birth see forms with the eye. And deaf beings hear sounds with the ear. And unconscious beings regain their mindfulness. And beings whose minds were distraught were no longer distraught in mind. (**9**) And naked beings became clothed in robes. And hungry beings became full-bellied. And thirsty beings became thirstless. And disease-afflicted beings became diseaseless. And beings whose bodily organs were defective became possessed of complete organs. On a large scale in the world there was an appearance of miraculous things.

Then when the Bodhisattva Ruciraketu saw those Lord Buddhas, he became amazed: "How is that (possible)?" Pleased, joyful, delighted, rejoicing, full of joy and gladness, he paid homage to where those Lord Buddhas were, and recollecting those Lord Buddhas according to their forms[(6)], recollecting the virtues of the Lord Śākyamuni, he began to be puzzled concerning the measure of life of the Lord Śākyamuni. He was revolving this reflection: "How is this (possible)? Why is it that the Lord Śākyamuni had such a brief measure of life as eighty years?"

Then indeed those Lord Buddhas, mindful (and) aware (of this thought) spoke thus to the Bodhisattva Ruciraketu: "Think not so, noble son, (that) the measure of life of the Lord Śākyamuni was so

[(6)] 'according to their forms' renders Sanskrit *ākārataḥ*. Cf. F. Weller, *OLZ*, 69, 1974, 388.

brief. Why is that? We[7] do not see anyone in the world of gods, Māras, Brahmas, among the race of ascetics and brahmins, gods, men and Asuras who would be able **(10)** to understand to the furthest end the limit of the measure of life of the Tathāgata, the Lord Śākyamuni, apart from Tathāgatas, Arhats, those fully enlightened."

And as soon as those Lord Buddhas had uttered (this) explanation of the measure of life of the Tathāgata, then by the power of the Buddha the gods residing in the realms of desire and of forms, including Nāgas, Yakṣas, Gandharvas, Asuras, Garuḍas, Kiṃnaras and Mahoragas, assembled, and numerous hundreds of thousands of millions of Bodhisattvas came together in the house of the Bodhisattva Ruciraketu. Then those Tathāgatas proclaimed in verses to the entire assemblies (this) explanation of the measure of life of the Lord Śākyamuni:

"The drops in all the oceans of water can be counted, but no one can count the life of Śākyamuni." **(11)**

"As far as the Sumeru mountains are concerned, all their atoms can be counted, but no one can count the life of Śākyamuni."

"However many atoms there are on earth it is possible to count them all but not to count the life of the Buddha."

"If anyone should wish to measure the sky, (it is possible), but no one can count the life of Śākyamuni."

"Let there be so many aeons and hundreds of millions of aeons, so many perfect Buddhas, yet the count (of his life) is not obtained."

"Because there are two causes for it and likewise two reasons: **(12)** refraining from evil injury and giving much food, therefore the count of the life of that great-souled one is not obtained in so many aeons, likewise in so many innumerable aeons."

"Therefore be free from doubt. Have no doubt at all. As for the limit of the Buddha's measure of life, its count is nowhere obtained."

Then indeed at that time in that assembly the teacher and expounder called Kauṇḍinya, a brahmin, together with numerous thousands of brahmins, did an act of homage to the Lord, and having heard the report of the Tathāgata's great complete Nirvāṇa[8], he at once fell in

[7] Read *vayaṃ* for *caivaṃ* Nobel, *Tib.* p.10 n.98.

[8] Cf. F. Weller, *OLZ*, 69.7/8, 1974, 388.

tears[(9)] before the Lord's feet and said to the Lord:

"If in fact the Lord is compassionate toward all beings, long-suffering, desirous of their welfare, the parent of all beings, unequalled, moon-like light-dispenser, risen like the great sun of wisdom and knowledge; if you look upon all beings as if upon (your son) Rāhula, grant me one boon."

The Lord remained silent.

(**13**) Then by the Buddha's power, in that assembly, Sarvalokapriyadarśana by name, a Litsavi prince, waxing eloquent, spoke thus to the teacher and expounder Kauṇḍinya: "Why ever do you, great brahmin, beseech the Lord for one boon? I myself grant it to you." The brahmin said: "For the sake of honouring the Lord, Litsavi prince, I wish to have a relic of the Lord the size of a grain of mustard, a particle of a relic for my possession. Thus it is heard: if one has honoured a relic the size of a grain of mustard, one obtains lordship over the Thirty-three gods. Listen, Litsavi prince, to the excellent Suvarṇabhāsasūtra, which is difficult (**14**) for all Śrāvakas and Pratyekabuddhas to perceive, difficult to understand. He will make manifest the excellent Suvarṇabhāsasūtra fully accompanied by such characteristics and virtues. Just so, o Litsavi prince, is the excellent Suvarṇabhāsasūtra difficult to perceive, difficult to understand, especially for us brahmins dwelling in borderlands. The relic the size of a grain of mustard is to be placed in a box. I beseech you for (this) boon that beings may very quickly obtain lordship over the Thirty-three gods. Why then, Litsavi prince, should one not wish to ask for a relic of the Tathāgata the size of a grain of mustard so that by placing it (and) depositing it in a box for relics one may obtain lordship over the Thirty-three gods for all beings? Thus, o Litsavi prince, I have asked for (this) boon."

Then Sarvalokapriyadarśana, the Litsavi prince, replied in verse to the teacher and expounder Kauṇḍinya, the brahmin:

(**15**) "When in the waters of the Ganges white lilies grow, (when) crows become red, cuckoos too the colour of the conch, (when) the

[(9)] 'in tears' is for Sanskrit *prarunda*, Skjærvø's emendation for MS. J *pururda*. *prarunda* corresponds to *braunde* 'he wept' in the Khotanese version and is reflected in the Chinese versions of Jñānagupta and I-Tsing.

rose-apple tree produces the fruit of the palm and the date-tree mango-blossoms, then a relic the size of a grain of mustard there will clearly be. When from tortoise-hairs there should be a well-made cloak removing the cold in winter, then there will be a relic. When from gnat's legs there should be a well-made tower, firm and unmoving, then there will be a relic. (**16**) When there arise in all leeches sharp, big, white teeth, then there will be a relic. When from hare's horns there should be a well-made ladder for the purpose of climbing up to heaven, then there will be a relic. When a mouse, having climbed up this ladder, should eat the moon and should vex Rāhu, then there will be a relic. When flies, having drunk a pot of wine, wander about the village and make their dwelling in a house, then there will be a relic. When the ass, possessed of a lip (red) as *bimba*-fruit, should be happy and skilled in dancing and singing, then there will be a relic. When the owl and the cow, having gone to a lonely place, should enjoy themselves together in mutual harmony, then there will be a relic. (**17**) When from the leaves of the *palāśa*-tree there should be a very firm umbrella for protection against the rain, then there will be a relic. When ocean-going ships fitted with oars and sails should ascend the dry land and proceed, then there will be a relic. When owls should go off taking in their beak the Gandhamādana mountain, then there will be a relic."[(10)]

When he had heard these verses, the teacher and expounder Kauṇḍinya, the brahmin, replied to Sarvalokapriyadarśana, the Litsavi prince, with the verses:

"Bravo, bravo, best prince, Buddha-son, great speaker, skilled in expedients, hero, best of those who have obtained a prophecy (to enlightenment). Listen to me, prince, concerning the inconceivable majesty, in due order, of the world's protector, the saviour, the Tathāgata. Inconceivable is the Buddha-sphere, and unequalled are the Tathāgatas. (**18**) All the Buddhas are always benevolent. All the Buddhas behave perfectly. All the Buddhas have the same appearance: this is the normal condition among Buddhas. This Lord Tathāgata is not created and has not arisen. His body that is as hard as the thunderbolt manifests his transformed body. And hence there is

[(10)] This set of verses may be compared with Jātaka iii 477.

nothing called a relic of the great sage even the size of a grain of mustard. How will there be a relic in a body without bone or blood? The depositing of a relic is by an expedient on account of the welfare of beings. For the one who has the Law as his body is the one fully enlightened; the sphere of the Law is the Tathāgata. Such is the Lord's body; such the exposition of the Law. This I heard and knew, for the boon was asked by me (and) the conversation was instigated by me for the sake of elucidating the truth."

Then indeed thirty-two thousand gods, having heard this profound explanation of the Tathāgata's measure of life, all raised their resolves to supreme and perfect enlightenment. The thoughts of their minds gladdened, with the sound of a united voice, they spoke the verse: **(19)**

"The Buddha does not enter complete Nirvāṇa (and) the Law does not disappear. For the ripening of beings does he teach complete Nirvāṇa. The Lord Buddha is inconceivable. The Tathāgata has an eternal body. He shows various manifestations by reason of the welfare of beings."

Then indeed the Bodhisattva Ruciraketu, having heard (this) explanation of the measure of life of the Lord Śākyamuni in the presence of those Lord Buddhas and of those two good men, was pleased, joyful, delighted, rejoicing, full of joy and gladness, and became filled with noble bliss. While this explanation of the measure of life of the Tathāgata was being given, the resolve of innumerable, incalculable (beings) was raised to perfect enlightenment. And those Tathāgatas disappeared.

So (ends) the second chapter, the Chapter on the Measure of Life of the Tathāgata, in the excellent Suvarṇabhāsa, king of sūtras. **(20)**

3. Chapter on Confession

Then indeed the Bodhisattva Ruciraketu slept. In the middle of his sleep he saw a golden drum, made of gold, shining everywhere just like the orb of the sun. And in all the directions he saw innumerable, incalculable Buddhas, sitting on beryl seats at the foot of jewelled trees, surrounded (and) honoured in an assembly of numerous hundreds of thousands, preaching the Law.

And there he saw a man with the form of a brahmin, beating that drum. There from the sound of the drum he heard these (and) similar confessional verses coming forth. (**21**) Then indeed the Bodhisattva Ruciraketu, as soon as he awoke, recollected these verses of confession of the Law. Having recollected them, at the end of that night he departed from the great city of Rājagr̥ha with numerous thousands of beings. He came to Mount Gr̥dhrakūṭa, where the Lord was, and having approached and worshipped the feet of the Lord with his head, he thrice walked round the Lord towards the right and sat down on one side. Sitting on one side, the Bodhisattva Ruciraketu made the respectful gesture with his hands towards the Lord and uttered those confessional verses that he had heard in the middle of his sleep from the sound of the drum:

"One night when I was not tired I fell asleep and saw a gleaming drum with a golden light everywhere. Shining like the sun it beamed everywhere. It glowed in the ten directions. I saw Buddhas everywhere. They were sitting on jewelled trees and on beryl seats[(II)] at the head of an assembly of numerous hundreds of thousands. (**22**) I saw one in the form of a brahmin beating the drum, and while it was being struck by him, these verses came forth:

'By the excellent drum of golden light let the woes in the triple-thousand world be suppressed, the woes in the evil states, the woes in the world of Yama and the woes of poverty here in the threefold world. And by this resounding of the sound of the drum may all troubles in the world be suppressed, may beings be without fear, free of fear just as great sages are without fear, fearless. Just as the great sages who know all in the cycle of existence are endowed with all the noble virtues, (**23**) so may men be oceans of virtues endowed with the virtues of meditation and the (seven) members of enlightenment. And by this resounding of the sound of the drum may all beings possess the voice of Brahma. May they touch the best enlightenment of Buddhahood. May they turn the pure Wheel of the Law. May they remain (living) for inconceivable aeons. May they preach the Law for the welfare of the world. May they destroy impurities, annihilate

[(II)] 'on beryl seats' corresponds to Khotanese *vīrulīnāṃ āysanāṃ vīra* and Tibetan *rin-chen bai-ḍū-rya-dag-gi khri-la*.

woes, suppress passion, likewise hatred (and) folly. May those beings who dwell in an evil state, their limbs alight with blazing fire, hear the sound of the drum. May they take up the refrain: "Homage be to the Buddha." May all beings be mindful of their (former) births during hundreds of births, thousands of millions of births. Continually mindful of the great sages, let them hear their word, for it is noble. **(24)** And by this resounding of the noise of the drum may they always obtain a meeting with the Buddhas. May they avoid evil action. May they practise meritorious acts of good. For those men, Asuras, all beings who have desires (and) wishes, may I fulfill them all by this resounding of the noise of the drum. For those beings who have taken birth in a fierce hell, their limbs alight with blazing fire, and, without protection and oppressed with grief, wander about, there will be quenching of their fires. Those beings whose woes are fierce[12] and terrible in hells, among ghosts (or) in the world of men, by this resounding of the noise of the drum, may all their woes be suppressed. And may I be for those who are without deliverance, without rescue, without refuge, the deliverer, the refuge, the excellent protector. **(25)** May the Buddhas, whose minds are (full) of mercy (and) compassion, watch over me, those best of the two-footed, who dwell in the world in its ten directions. And whatever evil, cruel act was done by me previously, I will confess it all before the Buddhas. Whatever evil I have done by not attending to my parents, by neglecting the Buddhas, **(26)** by neglecting the good; whatever evil I have done by being drunk with the intoxication of authority or with the intoxication of high birth or by being drunk with the intoxication of tender age; whatever evil I have done, bad thought, bad word, by an act badly done (or) by not perceiving a mishap; whatever evil I have done by the application of foolish reasoning, by a mind dark with ignorance, under the influence of an evil friend or by a mind distracted by impurities, under the compulsion of sport (or) enjoyment, or through the influence of anxiety (or) anger, (or) through the fault of unsatisfied wealth; whatever evil I have done by my associations with ignoble people, by reason of envy (and) greed, (or) by the fault of guile (or)

[12] 'fierce' for MS. J *pracaṇḍa* (Skjærvø) rather than Nobel's conjectured *dāruṇāś ca*.

wretchedness; (**27**) whatever evil I have done through failure to gain the mastery over my desires by reason of fear at the time of approaching troubles[(13)]; whatever evil I have done through the influence of a flighty mind or through the influence of passion (and) anger (or) through being oppressed by hunger and thirst; whatever evil I have done for the sake of drink and food, for the sake of clothing, for a reason involving women, through the various afflictions of impurities; whatever evil of body, tongue and mind, bad action accumulated in threefold manner, I have done, together with similar things, I confess it all. Whatever disrespect I may have shown to Buddhas, doctrines, likewise to Śrāvakas, I confess it all. Whatever disrespect I may have shown towards Pratyekabuddhas or towards Bodhisattvas, I confess it all. [(14)][If I have shown disrespect towards those who preach the Good Law or towards other meritorious beings, I confess it all.] If I have unawares continually rejected the Good Law (**28**) (or shown) disrespect towards my parents, I confess it all. (Whatever evil I have done) through stupidity or from folly or through being full of pride and arrogance, through passion, hatred or delusion, I confess it all.'

'I will worship the Buddhas in the ten directions in the world. I will deliver the beings in the ten directions from all woe. I will establish in the tenth stage all the inconceivably many beings. And when I have placed them in the tenth stage, may they all become Tathāgatas. May I follow my career for millions of aeons for the sake of every single being until I am able to deliver every one from the ocean of woe. May I expound to those beings this profound Confession. The excellent Suvarṇabhāsa by name causes the destruction of all acts. By proclaiming it once, all the cruel evil one has done in thousands of aeons pro-

[(13)] F. Weller proposed to render this sentence: '(Ich werde bekennen,) was ich Böses tat zu der Zeit, da Drangsal über uns kam, ich, der ich die Herrschaft nicht (über mich) gewann, von wegen der Schrecklichkeit der sinnlichen Begierden.' (*OLZ*, 69.7/8, 1974, 388-389).

[(14)] This verse is not original (Nobel). It is not found in the Chinese versions nor in Sanskrit MSS. ABCDEF. In G it is corrupt. The verse is cited in this form in the Śikṣāsamuccaya (ed. C. Bendall) p.162.

ceeds to destruction. (**29**) Having expounded[15] this Confession, the splendid, excellent Suvarṇabhāsa, by which is quickly obtained the destruction of obstructions due to past acts, (**30**) may I stand[16] in the tenth stage, in[17] the choice mine (made of) the ten jewels. May I shine with the Buddha-qualities[18]. May I make[19] (beings) cross over from the ocean of existence. And may I fill the flood of the Buddha-sea, the deep ocean of virtues, omniscience, with inconceivable Buddha-qualities[20]. May I become an excellent Buddha with hundreds of thousands of meditations, with inconceivable magic formulas, with the senses, with the (ten) powers (and) the (seven) members of enlightenment.'

'May the Buddhas watch over me with minds attentive. May they forgive my sin with minds given over to compassion. (**31**) On account of the evil done by me previously even in hundreds of aeons, I have a troubled mind oppressed with wretchedness, trouble and fear. With an unhappy mind I continually fear evil acts. Wherever I go there is no enjoyment for me anywhere. All the Buddhas are compassionate. They remove the fears of all beings. May they forgive my sin and may they deliver me from fear. May the Tathāgatas take away for me the defilement of impurities (and) acts. And may the Buddhas bathe me with the surging waters of compassion. I confess all the evil previously done by me and I confess all my present evil. For the future, I undertake to refrain from all acts evilly done. I do not conceal what-

(15) 'having expounded' is for Nobel's conjectured **deśayitvā*, with which the Tibetan *bśags-nas* agrees and which is clearly reflected in the Khotanese *khvaṃ hva yinī* 'when I have expounded to them'.

(16) 'may I stand' renders Sanskrit *sthāsyāmi*, with which Khotanese *viṣṭī* agrees.

(17) The use of the locative here reflects the Sanskrit MSS., which Nobel unjustifiably emended to accusative plural. Read *daśa-ratnākare vare*. The Khotanese also has a clear locative singular *ramna-vaṃdāya*.

(18) The Sanskrit MSS. ABCDEGJ have the instrumental plural *guṇais*.

(19) Sanskrit *tareyaṃ* seems here to be causative 'may I make cross'. Cf. F. Weller, *OLZ*, 69.7/8, 389. The Tibetan *bsgral-bar bgyi* indicates a causative as do the Khotanese renderings *nvāyīñä* 'may I convey' and *ttrāyākä ... himąne* 'may I become a conveyor'.

(20) The meaning of this sentence is unclear. Cf. F. Weller, *OLZ*, 69.7/8, 1974, 389.

ever evil I may have done. [21]The threefold bodily act and the fourfold with the voice, (**32**) as well as the act in three ways with the mind, all this I confess. What I have done with my body, what I have done with my voice, and what I have thought with my mind, the tenfold act I have done, I confess it all. May I avoid the ten evil acts. May I practise the ten good acts. May I remain in the tenth stage. May I become an excellent Buddha. Whatever evil act I have done bringing an undesired fruit I will confess it all in the presence of the Buddhas.'

'Those who in this Jambudvīpa and in other world-spheres do a good act I congratulate on it all. And whatever merit has been gained by me by body, voice or mind, through that merit-root may I touch excellent enlightenment.'

'In the oppression of existence (or) through foolish thought, whatever severe evil I have done, (**33**) in the presence of the Buddha, I confess all this evil. And I confess that evil which has been heaped up by me in the oppression of birth, by the various oppressions of activity due to passion[22], in the oppression of existence, in the oppression of the world, in the oppression of the fleeting mind, in the oppression of impurities caused by the foolish and stupid, and in the oppression of the arrival of evil friends, in the oppression of fear, in the oppression of passion, in the oppression of hatred and in the oppression of folly and darkness, (**34**) in the oppression of the opportunity, in the oppression of time, in the oppression of gaining merits, standing in (my) oppression before the Buddha, I confess all this evil.'

'I worship the Buddhas, who are like oceans of virtues, mountains gleaming with the colour of gold like Sumeru. I go for refuge to those Buddhas and with my head I bow down to all those Buddhas. (Each one is) gold-coloured, shining like pure gold. He has fine eyes, pure and faultless like beryl. He is a mine blazing with glory, splendour, and fame. He is a Buddha-sun removing the obscurity of darkness

[21] The reference is to the ten evil acts (see 51-52), which consists of three bodily acts, four with the voice and three with the mind (Mahāvyutpatti 1681-1684). For the list in Pāli, see *Encyclopaedia of Buddhism*, ed. G. P. Malalasekera, s.v. *akusala*.

[22] 'passion' renders the reading of the Sanskrit MSS. *kāma*, emended by Nobel to *kāya*. *kāma* is reflected by Khotanese *brrīvījau*.

with his rays of compassion. He is very flawless, very brilliant, with very gleaming limbs. He is a fully enlightened sun. His limbs are as prominent as pure gold. **(35)** He refreshes as it were the blazing fire of those whose minds are consumed by the fire of impurities with the sage's meshes of moonbeams. His sense organs are beautiful[(23)] with the thirty-two excellent major marks, his members greatly gleaming with the very brilliant minor marks. With meshes of beams full of glory, merits, splendour, and brilliance[(24)] he stands amid the darkness like the sun in the three worlds.

'Your members resembling silver, crystal or copper, with various magnificent colours pure as beryl, with meshes of rays manifoldly and variously adorned, coppery red like the dawn, you shine, great sage, like the sun. For one who has fallen into the river of the cycle of existence, in the midst of the flood of disaster, afflicted with anxiety, in the water of death, in the billow of old age, dry up[(25)] completely with the meshes of rays of the Budhha-sun the ocean of woe, whose current is extremely harsh and cruel.' **(36)**

'I worship the Buddha, whose members shine like gold, whose members gleam with the colour of gold, a mine of knowledge, chief in all three worlds, beautiful, whose members are adorned with very brilliant marks. Just as the water in the ocean is immeasurable, just as the earth is endless with its particles of dust, just as Meru is endless with its stones, just as the sky has an endless limit, so indeed are the Buddha's virtues endless. Even all beings cannot know them. If one should weigh and ponder them for numerous aeons, one could not know the last virtues. The earth with its rocks, mountains, and oceans, it is perhaps in aeons possible to count and know, and the water (in the ocean) may perhaps be measured to a hair-point: it is not possible to know the end of the Buddha's virtues.' **(37)**

'May all beings be such in virtue, appearance, fame, glory, with

(23) Read *lalita-* for *latita-* (misprint).

(24) Read *teja-jvalanākula-* for Nobel's *jvalanākula-*. The Sanskrit MSS. ABCDEFJ have *teja-*, and this is implied by Tib. I *gzi* and Khotanese *ttīśä'*. *jvalana* appears to be reflected by Khotanese *brūñąma* 'shining'.

(25) Read with Skjærvø *saṃśoṣaya* (2 sg. imper.), cf. MS. F *saṃtokhaya*. Khotanese *pahvąñarī* is also imperative.

body adorned with the beautiful major marks (and) decorated with the eighty minor marks. And by this good act, may I ere long become a Buddha in the world; may I preach the Law for the welfare of the world; may I deliver beings oppressed by many woes; may I overcome Māra with his might and with his army; may I turn the Wheel of the excellent Law; may I remain for inconceivable aeons; may I satisfy beings with the water of nectar; may I fulfill the six unrivalled perfections just as they were fulfilled by previous Buddhas; may I smite the impurities; may I destroy woes; may I extinguish passion, likewise hatred (and) folly. And may I be continually mindful of former births for hundreds of births, thousands of millions of births. May I constantly recollect the great sages. May I listen to their speech, for it is noble. **(38)** And by this good act, may I always find a meeting with the Buddhas; may I utterly avoid evil action; may I practise the good acts, mines of excellence.'

'Everywhere in the spheres of all beings may all the woes in the world be extinguished. May those beings whose senses are defective, whose limbs are deficient, all now become complete in senses. May those lying[26] in the (ten) directions who are diseased, powerless, whose body is injured, and who are without protection, all be delivered quickly from their disease, and may they obtain health, strength, and senses. May those beings who are in danger of being threatened or killed by kings, thieves, or scoundrels, who are troubled by hundreds of different fears, may all those beings who are oppressed and suffering[27] be delivered from those hundreds of extreme, very dreadful fears. May those who are beaten, bound and tortured by bonds, and situated in various troubles, **(39)** distracted by numerous thousands of labours, who have become afflicted by various fears and cruel anxiety, may they all be delivered from their bonds; may the beaten be delivered from the beaters; may the condemned be united with life; and may all those who have come upon troubles become free from fear. May those beings who are oppressed by hunger and

[26] Sanskrit *śayitā* (emended to *daśa* by Nobel) is reflected by Khotanese *śānaṃdā* 'lying'.

[27] Read *vyasanāgataduḥkhitā hi* with MSS. ABCDEF and the Śikṣāsamuccaya (J. W. de Jong, *IIJ*, XIV, 1972, 120).

thirst obtain a variety of food and drink. And may the blind see the various forms, the deaf hear delightful sounds, the naked obtain various garments, poor beings obtain treasures. And may all beings be blessed with abundant wealth, corn, and various jewels. May the experience of woe harm no one. May all beings be good-looking. May they have beautiful, gracious, auspicious forms and continually have a heap of numerous blessings. As soon as they think of them, may there be for them food and drink as they desire, great abundance, and merits, (**40**) lutes, drums, (and) pleasant-sounding cymbals, springs, pools, ponds, (and) tanks. As soon as they think of them, may there be for them lotus-ponds of blue and golden lotuses, food and drink, likewise clothing, wealth, gold, ornament of gems and pearls, gold, beryl, and various jewels. May there be no sounds of woe anywhere in the world. May there be not one being of opposing mien, and may they all be of noble aspect, creating light for one another. Whatever success there may be in the world of men, (**41**) may it arise for them at their thought. As soon as they think of them, may all their desires be fulfilled through their merit (and its) fruit. May there rain down three times from the trees perfume, garlands, unguent, clothing,[(28)] powder, various flowers. May the beings accept them (and) be joyful. May they do honour, inconceivable, to all the Tathāgatas in the ten directions, to the Bodhisattvas, to the Śrāvakas, to the pure, flawless, firm Law. May beings avoid the low states of existence. May they avoid the eight non-opportunities. May they obtain the supreme, chief opportunity. May they always obtain a meeting with Buddhas. May they always be highborn (and) (**42**) have their treasuries replete[(29)] with abundant wealth and corn. For numerous aeons may they be thoroughly adorned with beauty, complexion, fame (and) glory. May all women constantly become men, strong, heroic, intelligent, and learned. May they constantly proceed to enlightenment and be active in the six perfections. May they see the Buddhas in the ten directions, comfortably seated under excellent jewelled trees, sitting together on

[(28)] I have rendered Sanskrit *vāsaṃ* as 'clothing' in accord with Tibetan *gos* and Khotanese *vāsta*.

[(29)] 'replete' renders Sanskrit *samṛddha*, indicated by most of the MSS including J as well as by Tib. and Chinese. Cf. also R. Tsuchida, *CAJ*, 29, 1985, 120.

seats of precious beryl. May they hear them expounding the Law. The evil acts obtained by me, what I obtained previously in the oppressions of existences, whatever the evil acts bringing undesired fruits–may they all without remainder be destroyed. May all beings who dwell in the bondage of existence, bound with firm fetters by the fetters of the cycle of existence, (**43**) be delivered from their bondage by the hands of wisdom. May they be delivered from their woes. May they become Buddhas.'[30]

'Whatever beings here in Jambudvīpa and whatever also in other world-spheres perform various, profound merits, I congratulate them all on this merit. By this my congratulation on their merits (and) by the (merit) obtained (by me) through body, voice or mind, (**44**) may there be fruitful success for my resolve. May I touch supreme, flawless enlightenment.'

'Whoever worships and praises the Buddhas continually, with mind believing, pure, spotless, by means of this (Confession), which is praised (as a cause of) transfer of merit,[31] and abandons the evil states for sixty aeons, and whoever, men, women, brahmins, warriors, with these celebrated verses, will praise the sage, standing with hands in the gesture of reverence, will recollect (his) births in all existences[32], will have (his) body adorned with all members and with all senses, (will be) endowed with various merits (and) with virtues, and he will be continually worshipped as a king[33] among men. Such will he be in each place (of birth).'

'Not under one Buddha have they performed good, nor even under two, nor four, nor five, nor ten, but they in whose ear this Confession enters[34] have performed good under thousands of Buddhas.'"

[30] 'may they become Buddhas' renders Khotanese *ba'ysa himāṃde*. The Sanskrit *alupajā bhavantu* is corrupt.

[31] Sanskrit *pariṇāmana* means 'transfer of merit': see J. W. de Jong, *IIJ*, XIV, 1972, 120.

[32] For the recollection of former births as a reward see G. Schopen, *JIABS*, 6.1, 1983, 109-147. This passage is discussed on pp. 114 f.

[33] Read *rājaś* for Nobel's *rājaiś* (Skjærvø) as indicated by the Khotanese nominative *rre*.

[34] Khotanese *hīśtä* 'comes' agrees rather with a form of Sanskrit *praviś-* 'enter' as found in MSS. ABCDEF than with Nobel's conjectured *ninādiṣyati*. Skjærvø

So (ends) the third chapter, the Chapter on Confession, in the excellent Suvarṇabhāsa, king of sūtras. (**45**)

4. Chapter (called) "Abundance of Lotuses"

Then indeed the Lord spoke thus to the noble goddess Bodhisattvasamuccayā:

"Then indeed, noble goddess, at that time, at that moment, there was a king called Suvarṇabhujendra. With this praise of all the Tathāgatas (known as) 'Abundance of Lotuses' he praised the Lord Buddhas, past, future and present":

"Those Buddhas of former times, and those who are (now) and dwell in the ten directions in the world, I do worship to those Buddhas. I will praise all those Buddhas. (Each one is) an excellent sage, calm, composed, pure. His limbs shine with the colour of gold. The Buddha's voice is the best among all kinds of sounds. He has the Brahma-voice with the sound of thunder. (**46**) He has hair like a bee, a peacock, or a plant, blue, very curly, like the blue jay. His teeth are very white like a conch-shell or snow, continually shining, brilliant as gold. His eyes are blue, expanded, very flawless, blue like the colour of the blossoming blue lotus. His fine, broad tongue is like a lotus or gold, shining like a lotus, resembling a lotus-filament. He has a circle of hair on his face that resembles the conch or a lotus-fibre, turning to the right and the colour of beryl. The sage's eyes are fine like the waning moon, resembling the shining of bees. (**47**) His nose has a point, which is golden, soft as gold, high on his face, continually expanded. All the Buddhas have a taste, which is chief of all, excellent, best, always tender. He has excellent hair-pores for each hair. As soon as his fine hair emerges, it turns to the right. Shining like sapphire his plaited hair shone blue like the beautiful neck of a peacock[35]. His limbs shone at the moment of birth (and) filled all the worlds in the ten directions (so that) the endless woe in the three worlds was extinguished and beings were made content with every blessing. (**48**) In the hell-states, in the animal-states, and in the states of ghosts, of

sees *nipatiṣyati* behind J *nipratiṣyati*.

[35] For the rendering of this sentence see F. Weller, *OLZ*, 60.7/8, 1974, 389.

dwelling among the gods, of men, all the beings in their evil states were endowed with all blessings (and) becalmed. His limbs have the brilliance of the colour of gold and shine like refined gold. He has a face that is gentle like the moon,[(36)] pure as the moon, a countenance that is smiling, beaming, pure. He has members that are tender like the crescent (moon)[(37)]. He has tender limbs. His excellent, heroic gait is like a lion's. His dangling arms with their dangling hands are like creepers on the Śāl tree shaken by the wind[(38)]. **(49)** He sends forth a ray beaming and shining (the distance of) a fathom, blazing like a thousand suns. He is an excellent sage with choice, pure limbs, shining upon all the endless spheres. By reason of the shining of the brilliance of the Buddha the multitude of moons and suns in the endless hundreds of thousands of spheres all became lustreless. May (each) being see the Tathāgata-sun in the endless hundreds of thousands of spheres, the Buddha-sun, who is like a light to the world, among hundreds of thousands of Buddha-suns. (Each Buddha) has a body equipped with hundreds of thousands of merits, his limbs adorned with all the virtues. The Buddha's arm is like (that of) the best rutting elephant. The brilliance of his hands and feet is very bright and very pure. Equalling and resembling the dust on the earth's surface are those past Buddhas, who are (numerous) like the fine dust, and those who (will) arise (numerous) like the fine dust, and those who are (now, numerous) like the fine dust. To those Buddhas I do worship, faithful in body, voice, and mind, **(50)** with gifts of flowers and with gifts of fine perfumes, with a hundred praises and with a happy mind."

"Even with hundreds of tongues the Buddha's virtues cannot be told in thousands of aeons, for the virtues of the Buddhas, which have turned out well, are their essence, are excellent, various, numerous. And the virtues of a single Buddha cannot be stated with a thousand tongues. In any case it is impossible to tell the details of a single virtue of all the Buddhas. If the whole world including that of the

[(36)] Read *saumyaśaśāṅkasuvimalavaktram* with MSS. ABCDE (see J. W. de Jong, *IIJ*, XIV, 1972, 120.

[(37)] Cf. J. W. de Jong, *IIJ*, XIV, 1972, 120.

[(38)] For the interpretation of this sentence cf. F. Weller, *OLZ*, 69.7/8, 389-390.

gods should become an ocean full of water as far as the peak of existence, even so (the water) can be measured to a hair-point, yet not a single virtue of the Buddhas (can be measured). Praised, extolled by me are all the Buddhas with body, voice, and believing mind. (**51**) Whatever excellent fruits (there will be) of the merits accumulated by me, may beings thereby touch Buddhahood."

"When the king had thus praised the Buddha, he made the following resolve: 'Wherever birth may occur for me in endless future aeons, may I see such a drum in my dream, may I hear such a Confession there, may I obtain there in every birth such a eulogy of the Buddhas as the excellent "Abundance of Lotuses". May I hear in my dream the endless, peerless Buddha-virtues, which are hard to obtain even in thousands of aeons, and may I expound this during the day. May I deliver beings from the ocean of woe. May I fulfill the six perfections. (**52**) Afterwards may I obtain supreme enlightenment. May my sphere be without a rival. As a fruit of the fruition resulting from the presentation of the drum, and by reason of the praise of all the Buddhas, may I see face to face the Lord Śākyamuni. May I there receive the prophecy. These children, my two sons Kanakabhujendra and Kanakaprabha, may I obtain (together with) both children there, supreme enlightenment and the prophecy. (**53**) For those beings who are without dwelling, without protection, deprived of a refuge, and plunged in troubles, may I become in future time their protection, resort and refuge. As one who causes the destruction of arising woes and one who has become a mine of every blessing, may I proceed in a future aeon to enlightenment as so many previous millions have gone. By the exposition of the Suvarṇaprabhāsa may the ocean of evil be dried up for me; may the ocean of acts be destroyed for me; may the ocean of impurities be destroyed for me; may the ocean of merit be filled for me; may the ocean of knowledge be purified for me. By the excellent splendour of flawless knowledge may I become the ocean of all virtues. Filled with jewel-like virtues, with the virtues of enlightenment, by the power of the Suvarṇaprabhāsa and its Confession, may there be for me splendour of merits; may the splendour of enlightenment be pure for me. (**54**) By the excellent splendour of flawless knowledge may there be splendour of body for me. By the shining of the splendour of my merit may I become distinguished in the whole triple world. Continually endowed with the power of merit, a deliverer from the ocean of woe, and like a sea of all blessing, may I proceed to enlightenment in a future aeon. May[39] a field for me in future time be so distinguished by countless virtues as were the fields of all the Buddhas in the triple world distinguished by countless virtues, however many former millions of them passed.'"

So (ends) the fourth chapter, the Chapter called "Abundance of Lotuses", on the praise of all the past, future and present Tathāgatas, in the excellent Suvarṇabhāsa, king of sūtras.

(55) 5. CHAPTER ON EMPTINESS

Then indeed the Lord at that time uttered these verses:

"In inconceivably many other sūtras empty things have been expounded in great detail. Therefore these empty things are expounded briefly in (this) excellent sūtra. A being of slight intelligence, ignorant, is incapable of knowing all things. Therefore here in (this) excellent chief of sūtras the empty things are expounded briefly. By other expedients, methods, and causes, for the sake of producing the power of compassion for beings, **(56)** this excellent sūtra has been expounded so that all beings may understand. And this body is like an empty village. The senses are like six village thieves: they all dwell in the one village but they do not perceive one another. The eye-sense runs after forms, the ear-sense after the consideration of sounds, the nose-sense takes up various smells, the tongue-sense runs after tastes continually, the body-sense runs after sensations of touch, the mind-sense after consideration of things. These are the six senses, which severally approach their own object. **(57)** The mind is flighty like magic and the six senses consider their objects just as a man runs about in an empty village and is dependent on the six village thieves. So the mind, dependent on the six objects, knows fully the spheres of the senses, form, sound, likewise smell, taste, touch, likewise the sphere of things. And in the case of all six senses the mind, flighty like a bird, enters the senses and whatever sense it bases itself upon, it gives that sense its peculiar knowledge. And the body is motionless,

[39] Read *bheṣyatu* with MS G. The Tibetan also has an imperative here.

inactive, unsubstantial, having its origin through causes, (**58**) unreal, arising out of false discrimination. It is like a machine used by acts[40] (or)[41] like an empty village. Earth, fire, water, and wind, remaining in a village in various places, are always opposed to one another just like snakes in a single cage. And these snake-elements are fourfold: two are ascending, two descending. By twos they go in the directions and subdirections. All these snake-elements disappear. (**59**) The earth-snake and the water-snake both proceed downwards to destruction. The fire-snake and the wind-snake both are ascendant. Thought and perception, being dependent, having gone according to the action done previously among gods, men, and in the three evil states, have entered existence according to the act done. When the phlegm, wind and bile have attained their final destruction, the dead body is full of urine and excrement. (**60**) It gives no pleasure, having become a heap of worms. It is thrown down in a cemetery like a piece of wood. Behold these things, goddess. What here is a being or an individual? All these things are indeed empty and have arisen (only) by reason of ignorance. These great elements have great non-origination. Having originated from the unoriginated they are without origination. Therefore have they been proclaimed great elements by me, because having originated they are without origination. (**61**) By ignorance (*avidyā*) (a thing) is never found (*vidyate*), but it arises by reason of ignorance. Being thus not found and due to ignorance, therefore has this been called ignorance by me. Predisposition and consciousness associated with name and form, the six senses, contact, likewise feeling, desire, grasping, likewise arising of birth, old age and death, grief and affliction (constitute the chain of causation).[42] Inconceivable are the woes in the cycle of existence, and as they reside in the circle of existence, they have originated from the unoriginated, and (hence) they are without origination, without conception, (merely) the discrimination of the mind."[43]

[40] Cf. F. Weller, *OLZ*, 69.7/8, 1974, 390.

[41] The Khotanese has *o* 'or' here (24r5 *KT* 1.235).

[42] This is expounded in detail below (**193-94**).

[43] F. Weller renders this sentence thus: 'Die unausdenkbaren Leiden in der Wanderung durch immer neues körperliches Werden und wie es sich mit ihnen in

"Cut out the false view of self. With the sword of knowledge sever the net of afflictions. Regard the abode of the aggregates as become empty. Touch the noble virtue of enlightenment."

"I have opened the door of the City of Nectar. I have fully revealed the vessel of nectar juice. **(62)** I have entered the fair City of Nectar. I have sated myself with nectar juice. I have beaten the drum of the Good Law. I have blown the conch of the Good Law. I have lighted the lamp of the Good Law. I have rained down the rain of the Good Law. I have conquered the foreign enemies of afflictions. I have raised up the unmatched banner of the Law. I have rescued beings from the ocean of existence. I have closed the three paths to the evil states.[(44)] ... I have extinguished for beings the conflagration of the fire of their afflictions. ... Wherefore previously during numerous aeons I have honoured inconceivably many Leaders, I have proceeded by firm vow to enlightenment, seeking the body of the Good Law. **(63)** I gave up my hands and feet, wealth, gold, gems, pearls, ornaments, eyes, the supreme member (the head), beloved sons and daughters, gold, beryl and various jewels."

If one should cut up in the triple-thousand world from all the trees, grass and woods[(45)] ... and all of the tree; and if one should crush it all, make it like fine dust, making a heap of powder extending into the sphere of the sky, he is capable of analysing it into its three parts equal to the dust of the earth. ...[(46)] But even men with greater

diesem Kreise verhält, das ist alles, aus Unwirklichem hervorgegangen, ohne Wirklichkeit, nichts als ein Umtrieb der Gedanken.' (*OLZ*, 69.7/8, 1974, 390–391).

[(44)] Three lines seem to be missing from the Sanskrit of verse 25, as established by Nobel from comparison with the Tib. and Chinese. Tib. I reads: 'The beings have become consumed by the fire of afflictions (*kleśa*) and are without refuge, without protection. I have extinguished for creatures the conflagration of the fire of their afflictions (*kleśa*). I have satisfied them with cool nectar juice.'

[(45)] Verse 28 is apparently incomplete in the Sanskrit. Tib. I has: 'If one should cut into pieces all the trees in the triple-thousand world, all the grass and grasses, the woods and all that grows from the earth.'

[(46)] Verse 30 is incomplete in the Sanskrit and verse 31 is missing. Tib. I has: 'He is capable of analysing into its three parts here what is the dust on the earth, the inconceivable sphere of dust of all the triple-thousand worlds. (31) If the knowledge of every being should be present in one single being, with that knowledge one could count the particles of dust.'

knowledge than all beings are not able to count up all the knowledge of the Buddha. Whatever knowledge belongs to the Buddha in a single moment cannot at all be counted up in numerous millions of aeons.

So (ends) the fifth chapter, the Chapter on Emptiness, in the excellent Suvarṇabhāsa, King of sūtras. **(64)**

6. Chapter on the Four Great Kings

Then indeed the great king Vaiśravaṇa, the great king Dhṛtarāṣṭra, the great king Virūḍhaka, (and) the great king Virūpākṣa, getting up from their seats, put their cloaks over one shoulder, placed their right knees on the ground, and making a reverential gesture with their hands towards the Lord, they spoke thus to the Lord:

"Lord, this excellent Suvarṇabhāsa, king of sūtras, has been spoken by the Tathāgata, has been watched over by all the Tathāgatas, has been protected by all the Tathāgatas, has been taken care of by all the multitudes of Bodhisattvas, has been worshipped by all the multitudes of the gods, has been honoured by all the multitudes of the gods, has been praised by all the multitudes of the chief gods, has been honoured by all the world-protectors, has been praised, eulogised, extolled, **(65)** shines in the dwellings of all the gods, bestows supreme blessing on all beings, dries up all the woes of the hells, the animals, the world of Yama, allays all fears[(47)], repels all foreign armies, removes all the oppression of hunger, removes all the oppression of illness, overthrows all the planets, creates supreme tranquillity, removes grief and trouble, removes the various afflictions, destroys the hundreds of thousands of afflictions. When, dear Lord, this excellent Suvarṇabhāsa, king of sūtras, is being expounded in detail in the assembly, by merely hearing this Law and by the nectar juice of the Law, the divine bodies of us four great kings together with our armies and retinues will wax with great might. In our body there will be produced prowess, strength, and energy. Brilliance, glory and splendour will enter our body. We, dear Lord, the four great kings will be law-abiding, will preach the Law and will rule by the Law. By the Law,

[(47)] Read *sarvabhayapratiprasrambhaṇaḥ* (see J. W. de Jong, *IIJ*, XIV, 1972, 120).

dear Lord, will we exercise our sovereignty over the gods, Nāgas, Yakṣas, Gandharvas, Asuras, Garuḍas, Kiṃnaras and Mahoragas. We will rout the hordes of Bhūtas, who are pitiless, whose minds are without compassion, who take[(48)] their glory from others. **(66)** We, the four great kings, dear Lord, together with the twenty-eight great generals of the Yakṣas and with numerous hundreds of thousands of Yakṣas, will continually watch over, guard, and protect the whole of Jambudvīpa with our divine eye, which is pure and surpasses human eyes. For this reason, dear Lord, the name world-protector has been ascribed[(49)] to us four great kings. Whatever regions, dear Lord, in this Jambudvīpa will be smitten by a foreign army, will be oppressed by the affliction of hunger, by the affliction of illness, by hundreds of different oppressions, by thousands of oppressions, by hundreds of thousands of oppressions, we, dear Lord, the four great kings, will give encouragement to those monks who keep[(50)] the Suvarṇabhāsa, king of sūtras."

"And when, dear Lord, these monks, preaching the Law, by the magic power, influence and encouragement of us four great kings, approach those regions, they will proclaim in detail in those regions this excellent Suvarṇabhāsa, king of sūtras. These and similar various hundreds of thousands of oppressions afflicting those regions will cease. **(67)** Whichever region of a king of men, dear Lord, those monks who hold the chief sūtras and preach the Law shall enter, this excellent Suvarṇabhāsa, king of sūtras, will be brought to those regions. And when, dear Lord, a king of men should hear this excellent Suvarṇabhāsa, king of sūtras, and having heard it, should give protection, should give salvation, assistance, defence from all their enemies to those monks who hold the chief sūtras, we, dear Lord, the four great kings, will give protection, will give salvation, assistance, defence, peace, welfare to that king of men and to the beings in all regions. And when, dear Lord, the king of men should make blessed with the gift of every blessing those monks, nuns, laymen and lay-women who hold the chief sūtras, we, dear Lord, the four great kings,

(48) Read *anyatejasaharāṇi* Nobel, *Tib.* p.49 n.35.

(49) Read *saṃjñodapādi* (Skjærvø) for Nobel's *saṃjñotpāditā*.

(50) Deleting *ca sūtrendra* with Nobel, *Tib.* p.49 n.52.

will make blessed with all blessings and endowed with all commodities the beings in every district of that king of men." **(68)**

"And when, dear Lord, the king of men should honour, respect, reverence, worship the monks, nuns, laymen and laywomen who hold the chief sūtras, we, dear Lord, the four great kings, will make that king of men more honoured than all kings, and we will cause him to be respected, will cause him to be reverenced, will cause him to be worshipped, and will cause him to be praised in all regions."

Then indeed the Lord congratulated the four great kings: "Bravo, bravo, great kings! Bravo, bravo, you great kings! As you have rendered services to previous Buddhas, have planted merit-roots, have been honoured by many hundreds of thousands of millions of Buddhas, are law-abiding, preach the Law, and exercise sovereignty over gods and men according to the Law, as for a long time previously your minds have been devoted to the welfare, blessing, and love of all beings, you were endowed with a disposition to the welfare and blessing of all beings, you eliminated every discomfort, you were intent upon bringing complete welfare to all beings, (as) you, the four great kings, will give protection to those kings of men who are intent upon worship and honour to this excellent Suvarṇabhāsa, king of sūtras, will give salvation, assistance, defence, **(69)** peace, therefore the Way of the Law of the past, future and present Lord Buddhas will be protected, will be guarded and preserved by you, the four great kings, with your armies and retainers and with numerous hundreds of thousands of Yakṣas. Therefore there will be victory for you, the four great kings, together with your armies and retainers and numerous hundreds of thousands of Yakṣas, when you enter the conflict of the gods and Asuras. And there will be defeat for the Asuras. Thus, for the sake of this excellent Suvarṇabhāsa, king of sūtras, which overcomes all foreign armies, you will give protection, will give assistance, defence, peace, welfare to those monks, nuns, laymen and laywomen who hold the chief sūtras."

Then the great king Vaiśravaṇa, the great king Dhṛtarāṣṭra, the great king Virūḍhaka, and the great king Virūpākṣa, getting up from their seats, covered one shoulder with their cloaks, placed their right knees on the ground, and putting their hands in the gesture of reverence towards the Lord, they spoke thus to the Lord:

"Wherever, dear Lord, in future time this excellent Suvarṇabhāsa, king of sūtras, will go forth in villages, cities, settlements, districts, lands, royal palaces, and whichever king of men's region it may reach, whichever king of men, dear Lord, there may be who will exercise (**70**) sovereignty in accordance with the treatise on kingship (called) 'Instruction concerning Divine Kings', who will hear, reverence, honour this excellent Suvarṇabhāsa, king of sūtras, and will respect, venerate, reverence, honour those monks, nuns, laymen and laywomen who hold the chief sūtras and will continually listen to the excellent Suvarṇabhāsa, king of sūtras, by this flowing water of the hearing of the Law and by the nectar juice of the Law, he will magnify with great might these divine bodies of us four great kings with our armies and retinues and those of the numerous hundreds of thousands of Yakṣas. And he will produce in us great prowess, energy and power. He will magnify our brilliance, glory and splendour. Therefore we, dear Lord, the four great kings, with our armies and retinues and with numerous hundreds of thousands of Yakṣas, with invisible bodies, now and in future time, wherever we come upon villages, cities, settlements, districts, lands and royal palaces, there this excellent Suvarṇabhāsa, king of sūtras, (**71**) will go forth, and we will give protection, will give salvation, assistance, defence, escape from punishment, escape from the sword, peace, welfare to their royal palaces, their lands, and their regions. And we will deliver those regions from all fears, oppressions, (and) troubles. And we will turn back foreign armies."

"If there should be another hostile king neighbouring upon that king of men who hears, reverences, honours this excellent Suvarṇabhāsa, king of sūtras, and if, dear Lord, this neighbouring hostile king should produce such a thought: 'I will enter that region with a fourfold army to destroy it,' then indeed, dear Lord, at that time, at that moment, by the power of the brilliance of that excellent Suvarṇabhāsa, king of sūtras, there will arise a conflict between that neighbouring hostile king and other kings. And there will be regional disturbances in his own regions. (**72**) There will be fierce troubles with kings, and diseases caused by planets will become manifest in his area. Hundreds of different distractions will become manifest in his area. And if, dear Lord, there should arise for that neighbouring hostile king in his own area hundreds of such various oppressions and hundreds of various distractions, and (if), dear Lord, that neighbouring hostile king should employ his fourfold army to go against a foreign power and it should leave his own area, and (if) that hostile king together with his fourfold army should desire to enter, should desire to destroy that region where this excellent Suvarṇabhāsa, king of sūtras, may be, we, dear Lord, the four great kings, with our armies and retinues, with numerous hundreds of thousands of Yakṣas, with invisible bodies, will go there. We will turn back that foreign army from the very path it has taken. We will bring upon it hundreds of different distractions, and we will make obstacles so that that foreign army will not be able[51] to enter this region, much less cause destruction to the region."

Then indeed the Lord congratulated those four great kings: "Bravo, bravo, great kings! Bravo, bravo, again, great kings, since you will, (**73**) for the sake of that supreme and perfect enlightenment acquired through incalculable hundreds of thousands of millions of aeons, give protection, give salvation, assistance, defence, escape from punishment, peace, welfare to those kings of men who hear, reverence, and honour this excellent Suvarṇabhāsa, king of sūtras, and you will protect, endow with salvation, assistance, defence, escape from punishment, peace, and welfare, those royal palaces, those cities, those lands, and those regions, and you will deliver those regions from all fears, oppressions, and troubles, and you will turn back foreign armies, and you will exert zeal for the removal of quarrel, strife, hostility, and contention among the kings of men in the whole of Jambudvīpa, and since in this Jambudvīpa, that belongs to you, the four great kings, with your armies and retinues, the eighty-four thousand kings in the eighty-four thousand cities will rejoice in their own regions and will rejoice in the sovereignty over their own realm and in their own accumulation of objects and will not injure one another, will not cause injury to one another, will obtain kingship according to their own accumulation of former acts (**74**) and will be contented with the sovereignty over their own realm, will not harm one another, will not advance for the harm of regions, and if in this

[51] Read *śakṣyati* with MSS ACDE. Cf. R. Tsuchida, *CAJ*, 29, 1985, 122.

Jambudvīpa in the eighty-four thousand regions and cities the eighty-four thousand kings will have minds devoted to the welfare of one another, minds full of love and blessing, will rejoice with one another without quarrel, strife, hostility, and contention in their own regions–then this Jambudvīpa, that belongs to you, the four great kings, with your armies and retinues, will be flourishing, will be plentiful, will be happy, will be full of many people and men. And the earth will become mightier. The seasons, months, half-months, and years will all be associated with the proper time. Day and night, planets, asterisms, moon and sun, will move properly. **(75)** In due time showers of rain will fall down upon the earth. The beings in the whole of Jambudvīpa will become rich with every possession and grain. They will have great enjoyment and be without envy. They will be liberal. They will follow the path of the ten good acts. For the most part they will be born in the good state of heaven. The dwellings of the gods will become full of gods and divine sons. Whatever, great kings, kings of men there will be who will hear this excellent Suvarṇabhāsa, king of sūtras, will reverence and honour it, and (who) will give respect, veneration, reverence, and honour to those monks, nuns, laymen and laywomen who hold the chief sūtras, and (who) by reason of sympathy for you, the four great kings, with your armies and retinues and numerous hundreds of thousands of Yakṣas, will continually hear this excellent Suvarṇabhāsa, king of sūtras, with this flowing water of the hearing of the Law and with the nectar juice of the Law he will satisfy these bodies of yours and he will increase these your divine bodies with great might. He will produce in you great prowess, energy, and power. He will increase your brilliance, glory, and splendour. **(76)** To me, Śākyamuni, the Tathāgata, Arhat, perfectly enlightened one, that king of men will do inconceivable, great, vast, extensive homage. That king of men will do inconceivable, great, vast, extensive homage with all services to numerous hundreds of thousands of millions of past, future, and present Tathāgatas. Thereby will great protection be given to that king of men. Thereby to that king of men will be given protection, salvation, assistance, defence, escape from punishment, peace, and welfare. And great protection will be given, salvation, assistance, defence, escape from punishment, peace, and welfare will be given to his chief queen, the king's sons, the whole harem, and the whole palace. And all the deities dwelling in the palace will become mightier, more powerful, and endowed with inconceivable blessing and happiness. They will experience various pleasures. The cities, lands, and regions will be protected, will be guarded, will be unoppressed, (77) will be without enemies, will be unconquered by all foreign powers, without misfortunes, and without troubles."

When he had so spoken, the great king Vaiśravaṇa, the great king Dhṛtarāṣṭra, the great king Virūḍhaka, and the great king Virūpākṣa spoke thus to the Lord:

"If, dear Lord, any king of men should exist who should be desirous of hearing this excellent Suvarṇabhāsa, king of sūtras, should be desirous of giving himself great protection, should be desirous of giving great protection to his chief queen, princes, princesses, and his whole harem, (52)[should be desirous of giving] great, [inconceivable, supremely distinguished, unequalled peace (and) welfare,] to his whole palace, [should be desirous of increasing in this life great, inconceivable sovereignty, should possess inconceivable royalty, should be desirous of obtaining an unlimited heap of merit, should be desirous of protecting all his own regions, should be desirous of guarding them, should be desirous of wholly protecting all his own regions, should be desirous of guarding them, should be desirous of making his own region unoppressed, without enemies, undefeated by all foreign powers, without misfortune, and without trouble, that king of men, dear Lord, with his mind undistracted, with honour and respect, must do homage and listen to this excellent Suvarṇabhāsa, king of sūtras. In order to hear this excellent Suvarṇabhāsa, king of sūtras, that king of men must enter the chief palace. And having entered that(53) palace, he must sprinkle it well with water of various perfumes and bestrew it with various flowers. (**78**) In that place, when it has been well sprinkled with water of various perfumes and has been strewn with various flowers, a seat of the Law is to be provided,

(52) A complete folio is missing here. The text presented by Nobel is reconstructed on the basis of the Tibetan and Khotanese translations.

(53) Nobel, *Tib.* p.58 n.359 reconstructs *tatropasaṃkramya* rather than *upasaṃkramya* as in his Sanskrit text.

set up high (and) well adorned with various adornments. That place must be well adorned with various umbrellas, banners, and flags.] And that king of men must wash his body well, wear well-perfumed clothes, be clad in new and brilliant garments, be adorned with various ornaments. For himself a lower seat must be provided. When he has sat down on that seat, he must not be elated by his sovereignty. There he must not have passion for royal dominion. He must listen to this excellent Suvarṇabhāsa, king of sūtras, with a mind that is free from all pride, elation, and haughtiness. In the presence of that monk who is preaching the Law he must produce the thought that the monk is his teacher. The king of men must at that time, **(79)** at that moment, look with affection and kindness upon his chief queen, princes, princesses, and the whole group attached to the harem. With affectionate words he must converse with his chief queen, the prince and princesses. He must with affectionate words converse with the whole group attached to the harem. He must command (to be done) various acts of honour on account of hearing the Law. He must satisfy himself with inconceivable, unrivalled affection. He must be blessed with inconceivable affection and happiness. He must have happy senses. He must meditate on grasping the meaning of the self.[(54)] His self must be gladdened with great gladness. He must stand up before the preacher of the Law with great abundance of joy."[(55)]

When this had been said, the Lord spoke thus to the four great kings:

"At that time moreover, great kings, at that moment, the king of men must clothe himself wholly in white, light-coloured, new, brilliant garments, must adorn himself well with various ornaments and adornments, must obtain white umbrellas, must depart from that place with great royal power, with great display of royalty and taking various auspicious items. **(80)** He must go to meet that monk who is preaching the Law. Why is that? However many steps the king of men takes there, [so many hundreds of thousands of millions of Buddhas

[(54)] Read *ātmanaś ca mahārtha-lābha cintayitavyaḥ* with Skjærvø.

[(55)] Read *praharṣa-* for *prema-* Nobel, *Tib.* p.59 n.382.

will he propitiate][56], for so many hundreds of thousands of millions of aeons will he avoid the cycle of existence, so many hundreds of thousands of millions of palaces of Cakravartin-kings will he obtain. However many steps he will take there, he will increase[57] with inconceivable great royal power over so many present (rulers), for numerous hundreds of thousands of millions of aeons he will obtain exalted residences, divine palaces made of the seven jewels, he will obtain numerous hundreds of thousands of noble, divine and human palaces,[58] he will acquire[59] great dominion in all his births, he will be long-lived, he will reach old age, he will be eloquent, he will be of agreeable speech, he will be famous, he will have a very widespread reputation, hc will bc praiseworthy, he will be blessed in the world of gods, men, and Asuras. He will obtain the noblest blessings of gods and men. He will have great power. He will have the power and might of a great crowd and will be handsomc. He will be amiable and good-looking. He will have supreme magnificence of fair colour. In all his births he will meet with Tathāgatas. He will obtain every spiritual adviser. He will possess an unlimited heap of merit. O great **(81)** kings[60], seeing these and similar blessings (resulting) from virtues, the king must rise up a league before the preacher of the Law. He must rise up a hundred leagues, a thousand leagues (before him). In the presence of that preacher of the Law he must produce the thought that the preacher is his teacher."

"He must think thus: 'Today will Śākyamuni, the Tathāgata, Arhat, fully enlightened one, enter my palace here. Today will Śākyamuni, the Tathāgata, Arhat, fully enlightened one, in my palace here enjoy

[56] Translating Sanskrit *buddha-koṭi-niyuta-śata-sahasrāṇi ārāgayati*, which is not contained in the Sanskrit manuscripts but can be rcconstructed on the basis of the Tibetan, Chinese, and Khotanese versions: see P.O. Skjærvø, pp.246-247 of his article in *Iranian and Indo-European Studies, Memorial Volume of Otakar Klíma*, ed. P. Vavroušek, Praha 1994.

[57] Read *vivardhiṣyate* (1.6) Nobel, *Tib.* p.60 n.404.

[58] Read *rājakula-* for *rājaputra-* Nobel, *Tib.* p.60 n.406.

[59] Read *prāpto* (1.9) for *prāptaṃ* Nobel, *Tib.* p.60 n.409.

[60] Read *mahārājā guṇānuśaṃsāni* (see J. W. de Jong, *IIJ*, XIV, 1972, 120).

his food.[61] Today I will hear from Śākyamuni, the Tathāgata, the Arhat, the fully enlightened one, the Law, which is unacceptable to the whole world. Today by hearing this Law I will become a non-returner in supreme and perfect enlightenment. Today I will propitiate numerous hundreds of thousands of millions of Tathāgatas. Today I will do inconceivable, great, vast, extensive homage to past, future, and present Lord Buddhas. Today I will completely cut off all the woes of the hells, animalhood, and the world of Yama. Today I will plant the seeds of the merit-roots for numerous attainments of hundreds of thousands of millions of bodies with the sovereignty of Brahma-kings. Today I will plant the seeds of the merit-roots for numerous attainments of hundreds of thousands of millions of bodies in the position of Śakra. (**82**) Today I will plant the seeds of merit-roots for numerous attainments of hundreds of thousands of millions of bodies having the sovereignty of a Cakravartin-king. Today I will deliver from the cycle of existence numerous hundreds of thousands of millions of beings. Today I will obtain a heap of merit that is inconceivable, great, vast, extensive, unlimited. Today I will give great protection to the whole group of my harem. Today I will give here in the palace inconceivable, supreme, excellent, matchless, great peace, and welfare. Today I will protect my whole region. I will make it guarded, unoppressed, free of enemies, and undefeated by all foreign powers. I will make it free of misfortune and troubles.'"

"And if, great kings, that king of men, with this and similar reverence for the Good Law, should venerate, respect, worship, and honour those monks, nuns, laymen and laywomen who hold the excellent Suvarṇabhāsa, king of sūtras, (**83**) should give the best share (of the merit so acquired) to you, the four great kings, with your armies and retinues, to the multitudes of gods, and to numerous hundreds of thousands of Yakṣas, then that king of men, by the accumulation of merits and by the accumulation of good, will prosper with regard to his body and his present, inconceivable, great, royal dominion. He will be endowed with present, inconceivable, great, royal splendour. He will be adorned with glory, brilliance, and

[61] Read *bhojanam upabhokṣyati* for *svajanam anuśākṣyati* Nobel, *Tib.* p.61 n.425.

splendour. All his adversaries and all his enemies will be thoroughly overcome in accordance with the Law."

When he had spoken thus, the four great kings said this to the Lord:

"If there should be, dear Lord, a king of men who should hear this excellent Suvarṇabhāsa, king of sūtras, with this and similar reverence for the Law and he should venerate, revere, respect, and worship those monks, nuns, laymen and laywomen who hold the chief sūtras, (if) he should thoroughly purify his palace for the sake of us four great kings, (if) he should thoroughly sprinkle it with water of various perfumes, (**84**) (if) he should hear this Law together with us, the four great kings, (if) for his own sake and for that of all the gods he should give away even only a small share of merit, (if), dear Lord, for the sake of us four great kings, that king of men should, immediately after the monk who is preaching the Law has come to the seat of the Law and sat down, cause the spread of various perfumes, as soon as he has caused the various perfumes to spread, dear Lord, for the sake of honouring this excellent Suvarṇabhāsa, king of sūtras, creepers having various perfumes and odours will come forth. At that very moment, instant, second, in the sky above the several palaces of us four great kings there will arise umbrellas of creepers of various perfumes and odours. They will smell exalted perfumes. Gold-coloured lights will shine. And with that light our dwellings will be lit up. And there will arise umbrellas of creepers of various perfumes and odours. They will smell exalted perfumes. Gold-coloured lights will shine. And with that light our dwellings will be lit up. And there will arise umbrellas of creepers of various perfumes and odours, arriving[(62)] at that instant, moment, second, in the sky above the several palaces, dear Lord, of Brahma, lord of the world-sphere, of Śakra, king of the gods, of Sarasvatī, the great goddess, (**85**) of Dṛḍhā, the great goddess, of Śrī, the great goddess, of Saṃjñāya, great general of the Yakṣas, of the twenty-eight great generals of the Yakṣas, of Maheśvara, the divine son, of Vajrapāṇi, great general of the Yakṣas, of Māṇibhadra, great general of the Yakṣas, of Hārītī with her retinue of five hundred sons, of Anavatapta, the great king of the Nāgas, and

[(62)] Reading *°bhavanānāṃ kṣaṇalavamuhūrtenopary antarīkṣeṇāgatya nānā°* Nobel, Berichtigungen.

of Sāgara, the great king of the Nāgas. And they will smell the various exalted perfumes. And gold-coloured lights will become visible[63] inside their dwellings. With this light all their dwellings will be lit up."

When this had been said, the Lord spoke thus to the four great kings:

"Not only will there arise umbrellas of creepers of various perfumes and odours in the sky above the dwellings of you, great kings, the four great kings. **(86)** Why is that? As soon, great kings, as those various perfumes have been spread by that king of men for the sake of honouring this excellent Suvarṇabhāsa, king of sūtras, and creepers of various perfumes and odours arise from the one perfume-spoon that he has taken in his hand, then at that very moment, instant, second, in this whole triple-thousand great-thousand world-sphere, in which there are a hundred million moons, suns, great oceans, Sumerus, kings of mountains, Cakravāḍas and Mahācakravāḍas, kings of mountains, world-spheres of four great continents, gods belonging to the group of gods of the four great kings, Thirty-three gods, Yāma-gods, Tuṣita-gods, Nirmāṇarati-gods, Paranirmitavaśavartin-gods, gods dwelling in the stage of the endlessness of space, gods dwelling in the stage of the endlessness of consciousness, gods dwelling in the stage of nothingness, gods dwelling in the stage of neither consciousness nor unconsciousness, among all these in this triple-thousand great-thousand world-sphere, **(87)** among hundreds of millions of groups of Thirty-three gods and in the sky above the several dwellings of all the groups of gods, Nāgas, Yakṣas, Gandharvas, Asuras, Garuḍas, Kiṃnaras, and Mahoragas, those umbrellas of creepers of various perfumes and odours will arise. And they will smell exalted perfumes. In the dwellings of all the gods gold-coloured lights will become visible. And with that light the dwellings of all the gods will be lit up. And just as in the sky above the dwellings of all the gods in the triple-thousand great-thousand world-sphere those umbrellas of creepers of various perfumes and odours will arise, so, great kings, by the power of the brilliance of this excellent Suvarṇabhāsa, king of sūtras, **(88)** as soon as the various perfumes have been spread by the king of men for

[63] Read *prādurbhaviṣyanti* Nobel, *Tib.* p.64 n.521.

the sake of honouring this excellent Suvarṇabhāsa, king of sūtras, creepers of various perfumes will come forth. At that moment, instant, second, on all sides in the ten directions in numerous world-spheres in as many hundreds of thousands of millions of Buddha-fields as there are grains of sand in the Ganges river, there will arise umbrellas of creepers of various perfumes and odours in the sky above as many hundreds of thousands of millions of Tathāgatas as there are grains of sand in the Ganges river. And among those numerous hundreds of thousands of millions of Buddhas they will smell various exalted perfumes and odours. Gold-coloured lights will become visible. And with that light those numerous hundreds of thousands of millions of Buddha-fields as many as the grains of sand in the Ganges river will be lit up. As soon, great kings, as these and similar great miracles have become manifest, those numerous hundreds of thousands of millions of Tathāgatas as many as the grains of sand in the river Ganges will think of that preacher of the Law, and they will congratulate him: 'Bravo, bravo, good fellow! Bravo again, you good fellow, (**89**) since you are desirous of making known in detail in this way this excellent Suvarṇabhāsa, king of sūtras, whose meaning is so profound, whose lustre is so deep, which is so endowed with inconceivable virtues. And those beings will not be endowed with a lesser merit-root who merely hear this excellent Suvarṇabhāsa, king of sūtras, much less those who take it up, hold it, recite it, understand it, and expound it in detail in the assembly. Why is that? As soon, good fellow, as they hear this excellent Suvarṇabhāsa, king of sūtras, numerous hundreds of thousands of millions of Bodhisattvas will become non-returners in supreme and perfect enlightenment.'"

Then indeed those numerous hundreds of thousands of millions of Tathāgatas on all sides in the ten directions in as many hundreds of thousands of millions of Buddha-fields as there are grains of sand in the river Ganges, established each in his Buddha-field, at that time, at that moment, with one speech, with one voice, with one resounding sound, spoke thus to that monk who was preaching the Law on the seat of the Law:

"You will come, good fellow, in future time to the seat of enlightenment. You will exhibit, good fellow, atop the excellent seat of enlightenment, sitting at the foot of the king of trees, attainments of the powers of vows and austerities, **(90)** blessed blessings, numerous hundreds of thousands of millions of difficult acts, the most distinguished in the whole triple world, surpassing those of all beings. You will thoroughly adorn, good fellow, the seat of enlightenment. You will deliver, good fellow, all the triple-thousand world-spheres. Sitting at the foot of the king of trees, good fellow, you will defeat the inconceivable army of Māra, of very terrifying aspect, of supremely frightening appearance, of variously disfigured form. On top of the excellent seat of enlightenment, good fellow, you will attain perfect enlightenment that is unequalled, calm, pure, profound, supreme. Seated, good fellow, upon the diamond seat that is firm in its noble strength, you will turn the Wheel of the supreme Law, which has been praised by all the Buddhas, supremely profound, twelvefold.[64] You will strike, good fellow, the supreme drum of the Law. You will blow, good fellow, the supreme conch of the Law. You will raise, good fellow, the great banner of the Law. You will light, good fellow, the supreme lamp of the Law. You will rain down, good fellow, the supreme great rain of the Law. You will defeat, good fellow, **(91)** numerous hundreds of thousands of afflictions. You will rescue, good fellow, numerous hundreds of thousands of millions of beings from the very terrifying ocean of great fear. You will deliver, good fellow, numerous hundreds of thousands of millions of beings from the wheel of the cycle of existence. You will propitiate, good fellow, numerous hundreds of thousands of millions of Buddhas."

When this had been said, the four great kings spoke thus to the Lord:

"Out of compassion, dear Lord, for the king of men, who, seeing these and similar present and future virtues in this excellent Suvarṇabhāsa, king of sūtras, has planted merit-roots under thousands of Buddhas, and seeing his acquisition of an unlimited heap of merit, we, dear Lord, the four great kings, with our armies and retinues, together with numerous hundreds of thousands of Yakṣas, while in our own dwellings, as soon as we have been impelled by the umbrellas of creepers of various perfumes and odours, will with invisible bodies

[64] Alluding to the twelve items in the chain of causation, on which see **(193-194)**.

approach for the hearing of the Law the palace of that king of men, which has its halls free of swept up dust, well cleaned, well sprinkled with water of various perfumes, adorned thoroughly with various adornments. Brahma, lord of the world-sphere, Śakra, king of the gods, Sarasvatī, the great goddess, Śrī, the great goddess, Dṛḍhā, the earth-goddess, Saṃjñāya, the great general of the Yakṣas, the twenty-eight great generals of the Yakṣas, Maheśvara, the divine son, Vajrapāṇi, lord of the Yakṣas, Māṇibhadra, the great general of the Yakṣas, Hārītī, with her retinue of five hundred sons, Anavatapta, the king of the Nāgas, Sāgara, the king of the Nāgas, and numerous hundreds **(92)** of thousands of millions (of gods) with invisible bodies (will approach for the hearing of the Law)[(65)] the palace of the king of men, which has been adorned[(66)] thoroughly with various adornments, where there will[(67)] have been provided for the preacher of the Law a seat of the Law thoroughly adorned with various adornments and set high upon the flower-strewn earth. We, dear Lord, the four great kings, with our armies and retinues, with numerous hundreds of thousands of Yakṣas, will be in agreement with all those. As soon as we have been satisfied by this nectar juice of the Law from the giver of the gift of the supreme, great Law, to the king of men who has as companion a spiritual adviser, who causes the attainment of good, we will give protection to that king of men. We will give deliverance, assistance, defence, peace, and welfare. And we will give protection to his palace, city, and region. We will give deliverance, assistance, defence, peace, and welfare. And we will deliver that region from all oppressions, misfortunes and troubles."

"If, dear Lord, there should be any king of men into whose region this excellent Suvarṇabhāsa, king of sūtras, should come, and if, dear Lord, this king of men should not respect, reverence, honour those monks, nuns, laymen and laywomen who hold the excellent Suvarṇabhāsa, king of sūtras, should not satisfy, not duly reverence with this hearing of the Law, this nectar juice of the Law, us, the four great

(65) Nobel, *Tib.* p.69 n.650 *tenopasaṃkramayiṣyāmo* for *tatra* (1.4), but 3 pl. is required.

(66) Read *nānālaṃkāra-* (with short final *a*) Nobel, Berichtigungen.

(67) Read *prajñaptaṃ bhaviṣyati* Nobel, *Tib.* p.68 n.649.

kings, and the numerous (**93**) hundreds of thousands of millions of Yakṣas, should not increase with great might these our divine bodies, should not produce in us prowess, energy, and power, should not increase in our bodies the brilliance, glory, and splendour, we, dear Lord, the four great kings, with our armies and retinues, with numerous hundreds of thousands of millions of Yakṣas, will neglect this region. When we, dear Lord, neglect the region, the groups of gods dwelling in all regions will neglect this region. When the gods, dear Lord, neglect the region, there will arise in that region various regional disturbances. There will be fierce disputes among kings. The beings in all the regions will become quarrelsome. They will become argumentative and contentious. They will enter a dispute. Various illnesses due to planets will become manifest in their region. From the various directions there will become manifest showers of meteors. Planets and asterisms will become at variance with each other. Images of the sun will be seen at the rise of the moon. (**94**) There will be eclipses of the moon and eclipses of the sun. In the midst of the sky the sun and the moon will be continually afflicted by Rāhu. At all times halos the colour of rainbows[(68)] will be visible in the sky. There will be earthquakes. The wells in the earth, disappearing, will dry up. Rough winds will blow in the region. Fierce rains will arise. There will be oppressions by hunger in the region. Foreign powers will destroy the region. [The region will be uprooted and those beings] will have much trouble.[(69)] [That region will be in an unhappy state.[(70)]] When, dear Lord, we, the four great kings, with our armies and retinues, with numerous hundreds of thousands of Yakṣas, and the groups of gods dwelling in the regions, neglect that region, there will arise in that region hundreds of these and similar variegated oppressions or thousands of oppressions."

"If, dear Lord, there should be any king of men who should be desirous of gaining great protection for himself, should be desirous of

(68) Read *indracāpa-* for *ulkāpāta-* Nobel, *Tib.* p.70 n.703.

(69) Following Nobel, *Tib.* p.70 n.710 *tāni ca sattvāny āyāsabahulāni bhaviṣyanti* instead of *teṣāṃ ca sattvānām āyāsabahulaṃ bhaviṣyati.* The beginning of the sentence is reconstructed by Nobel from Tib. I.

(70) Translating the Tibetan, as this sentence is missing in Sanskrit.

long experiencing various royal blessings, should be desirous of exercising his sovereignty with a mind given over to every blessing, should be desirous of making happy the beings in all regions, should be desirous of defeating all foreign armies, should be desirous of protecting his whole region for a long time, **(95)** should be desirous of exercising his sovereignty according to the Law, should be desirous of delivering his region from all fears, oppressions, misfortunes, and troubles, then that king of men, dear Lord, must assuredly hear this excellent Suvarṇabhāsa, king of sūtras. He must respect, venerate, reverence, and honour those monks, nuns, laymen and laywomen who hold the chief sūtras. We, the four great kings, with our armies and retinues, must be fully satisfied with this heaping up of merit-roots resulting from the hearing of the Law, with this nectar juice of the Law. And these our divine bodies must be increased with great brilliance.[(71)] Why is that? Because, dear Lord, that king of men must assuredly hear this excellent Suvarṇabhāsa, king of sūtras. However many, dear Lord, various mundane and supramundane treatises have been expounded by the lord Brahma, however many various treatises have been expounded by Śakra, king of the gods, however many various mundane and supramundane treatises have been expounded for the sake of beings by various seers who possess the five kinds of supernatural knowledge, [this excellent Suvarṇabhāsa, king of sūtras, is superior and more outstanding.[(72)]] Dear lord, superior to and more outstanding than the hundreds of thousands of Brahma-lords, numerous hundreds of thousands of millions of Śakras, and all the hundreds of thousands of millions of seers possessing the five kinds of supernatural knowledge is the Tathāgata, who for the sake of beings expounds in detail this excellent Suvarṇabhāsa, king of sūtras, **(96)** so that the kings of men in the whole of Jambudvīpa will exercise their sovereignty, that all beings will be blessed, [that one's own region will be protected, guarded[(73)]], that all regions will be un-oppressed, free from enemies, that all foreign powers will be defeated

[(71)] Read *mahātejasā* for *mahātaujasā* Nobel, Berichtigungen.
[(72)] Reconstructed from the Tibetan by Nobel.
[(73)] Reconstructed from the Tibetan by Nobel. He later preferred *paripālitaś* to *parigṛhītaś* (Berichtigungen).

and turned back, that those regions will becomc free from misfortunes, free from troubles, that the Law in every region will be free from trouble, undefeated, that the great lamp of the Law will be kindled and lit by those kings of men in their several regions, that the dwellings of all the deities will be filled with gods and divine sons, that we, the four great kings, with our armies and retinues, and the numerous hundreds of thousands of Yakṣas, and the multitudes of gods in the whole of Jambudvīpa will be satisfied and propitiated, [that these our divine bodies will increase in brilliance,(74)] that there will be produced in our body great prowess, strength, and energy, that brilliance, glory, and splendour will enter our body in greater measure, that the whole of Jambudvīpa will become plentiful, happy, and full of many people and men, that the beings in the whole of Jambudvīpa will be blessed, will experience various pleasures, that beings (**97**) during numerous hundreds of thousands of millions of aeons will experience inconceivable, most exalted blessings, will have meetings with the Lord Buddhas, and in future time will be fully enlightened in supreme and perfect enlightenment. All this now (is) duc to thc Lord, thc Tathāgata, the Arhat, thc fully enlightened one, (for) with great blessing from the power of compassion [surpassing hundreds of thousands of millions of Brahma-lords(75)], with the Tathāgata-knowledge that is unmatched and surpasses the divine knowledge of hundreds of thousands of millions of Śakras, (and) with the blessing from asceticism surpassing various numerous hundreds of thousands of millions of groups of seers all possessing the five kinds of higher knowledge, the Lord, the Tathāgata, the Arhat, the fully enlightened one, has in detail expounded here in Jambudvīpa this excellent Suvarṇabhāsa, king of sūtras, for the sake of all beings. Whatever mundane of supramundane royal duties, royal textbooks, and royal acts have gone forth in the whole of Jambudvīpa, by which these beings will be blessed, all those have been revealed, expounded, and set forth here in the excellent Suvarṇabhāsa, king of sūtras, by the Lord, the Tathāgata, the Arhat, the fully enlightened one. (**98**) For this

(74) Reconstructed by Nobel from the Tibetan and from parallel passages. Read *mahātejasā* (Berichtigungcn).

(75) Reconstructed from thc Tibetan by Nobel.

reason, dear Lord, for this cause, the king of men must assuredly hear respectfully, honour respectfully, and worship respectfully this excellent Suvarṇabhāsa, king of sūtras."

When this had been said, the Lord spoke thus to the four great kings:

"Therefore the four great kings with their armies and retinues will assuredly show great zeal for the sake of protecting those kings of men who hear, reverence, and honour this excellent Suvarṇabhāsa, king of sūtras. And, o great kings, they will sustain those monks, nuns, laymen and laywomen who hold the chief sūtras and the acts of the Buddha. They will perform Buddha-acts here in this world of gods, men, and Asuras. **(99)** They will expound in detail this excellent Suvarṇabhāsa, king of sūtras. Assuredly you, the four great kings, must give protection, must give defence, deliverance, assistance, peace, and welfare to those monks, nuns, laymen and laywomen who hold the chief sūtras so that the monks, nuns, laymen and laywomen who hold the chief sūtras may be protected, unoppressed, without misfortunes or troubles, happy-minded, in order to explain in detail to beings this excellent Suvarṇabhāsa, king of sūtras(76)."

Then indeed the great king Vaiśravaṇa, the great king Dhṛtarāṣṭra, the great king Virūḍhaka, (and) the great king Virūpākṣa, rose from their seats, covered one shoulder with their robes, put on their upper garment, placed their right knee on the ground, placed their hands in the gesture of reverence in the direction of the Lord, bowed down, and at that time, face to face, praised the Lord with these becoming verses:

"Buddha, (your) body is pure as the moon. Buddha, (you have) the brilliance of the rays of a thousand suns. Buddha, (your) eyes have the pure brilliance of the lotus. Buddha, (your) excellent teeth are flawless as lotus-fibres. Buddha, (your) virtues are like the ocean, a mine of numerous jewels. Buddha, (you are like) the ocean full of the water of knowledge, replete with hundreds of thousands of meditations. Buddha, (your) feet bear the mark of the wheel,(77) whose felly is all-embracing and which has a thousand spokes. (Your) hands and feet

(76) On the syntax of this sentence see R. Tsuchida, *CAJ*, 29, 1985, 126-127.

(77) The second major mark (*lakṣaṇa*). See also (**204**).

are adorned with a net.[78] The net on (your) feet is like (that on the feet of) a lord of geese. (We worship you), Buddha, (as) the lord of mountains, pure as gold, like the golden mountain. **(100)** Buddha, we worship (you as) the lord of mountains, (you), Buddha, who have all the virtues like Meru. We worship (you), purest Buddha, who are equal to the sky, resembling the moon, like the moon (reflected) in the water, the Tathāgata-moon, resembling illusion or a mirage."

Then indeed the Lord addressed the four great kings in verses:

"This best king of sūtras, the excellent Suvarṇabhāsa of the ten-powered Buddhas must be protected with firmest vigour[79] by you world-protectors. Since this jewel-like sūtra is profound and gives blessing to all beings may it long go forth in this Jambudvīpa for the sake of the welfare and blessing of beings. By it in the triple-thousand great-thousand world-sphere all the woes of the evil states, the woes of beings in hell, are removed. And here in Jambudvīpa may all the kings in Jambudvīpa, with great joy in their hearts, protect their regions according to the Law. By it this Jambudvīpa may become peaceful, plentiful, and enjoyable (and) all beings in the whole of Jambudvīpa will be blessed. This king of sūtras must be listened to by that king of men who has affection for his domain, affection for the welfare of himself, and affection for his royalty and dominion. This king of sūtras causes the destruction of foreign enemies, routs foreign armies, **(101)** removes the greatest fears and misfortunes, causes the greatest good. Like the jewel-tree that gleams, produces all virtues and stands in a good house, so this king of sūtras must be viewed by those who desire the virtues of the kings. Just as one who is oppressed by heat finds in cold, icy water relief from thirst, so may this king of sūtras provide the lords of men with virtues and blessings. Like a jewel-box in the palm of the hand, which is a mine of every jewel, so is the excellent Suvarṇabhāsa, king of sūtras, to multitudes of kings. This king of sūtras has been honoured by multitudes of gods, paid homage to by the king of the gods and protected by the four world-protectors, who possess great magic powers. For this king of sūtras

[78] The sixth major mark (*lakṣaṇa*).

[79] Skjærvø conjectures **su-dṛḍha-vīryaiḥ* on the basis of the corrupt reading in J *sadṛrdvavālyaḥ* corresponding to Tibetan *brćon-hgrus rab-tu brtan-pas*.

has been continually watched over by the Buddhas in the ten directions. The fully enlightened ones congratulate one who expounds this sūtra. Hundreds of thousands of Yakṣas protect the region in the ten directions (where) they hear this king of sūtras with joyful mind, happy. There are inconceivable multitudes of gods in Jambudvīpa. May all these multitudes of gods hear this sūtra joyfully. Through hearing this Law they obtain mighty brilliance and prowess, and they will cause to increase with great might their divine bodies."

Then indeed when the four great kings had heard these and similar verses in the presence of the Lord, they became amazed, astonished, delighted.[80] **(102)** Impelled in just a moment by the force of the Law, they shed tears. With their bodies erect, with all their limbs quivering, endowed with inconceivable joy, happiness, and gladness, they bestrewed the Lord with divine *māndārava*-flowers. Having bestrewed and scattered them, they rose up from their seats, covered one shoulder with their robes, placed their right knees on the ground, made the gesture of reverence in the direction of the Lord and spoke thus to the Lord:

"We, dear Lord, the four great kings, each king with his retinue of five hundred Yakṣas, will be continually attached to the monk who preaches the Law for the sake of honouring and protecting that preacher of the Law."

So (ends) the sixth chapter, the Chapter on the Four Great Kings, in the excellent Suvarṇabhāsa, king of sūtras.

7. Chapter on Sarasvatī [81]

Then indeed Sarasvatī, the great goddess, covered one shoulder with her robe, placed her right knee on the ground, made the gesture

[80] Read *audbilyaprāptās* for Nobel's *udvignaprāptās*. The MSS. indicate this reading as does the Tib. Moreover, the cliché is well known. See e.g. É. Lamotte, *L'Enseignement de Vimalakīrti (Vimalakīrtinirdeśa)*, Louvain 1962, p.105 n.45.

[81] For a detailed discussion of this chapter see J. Nobel, 'Das Zauberbad der Göttin Sarasvatī', pp. 123-239 in *Festschrift Schubring*, Hamburg 1951. See also D. Maue and O. Sertkaya, 'Drogenliste und Dhāraṇī aus dem "Zauberbad der Sarasvatī" des uigurischen Goldglanzsūtra (Teil I)', *Ural-Altaische Jahrbücher*, Neue Folge Band 6, 1986, 76-99.

of reverence in the direction of the Lord and spoke thus to the Lord:

"I, dear Lord, the great goddess Sarasvatī, will contribute eloquence for the sake of adorning the speech of the monk who preaches the Law. (**103**) And I will bestow on him a dhāraṇī. I will arrange the substance of his speech so that it is well spoken. I will give great illumination of knowledge to the monk who preaches the Law. Whatever words or letters from this excellent Suvarṇabhāsa, king of sūtras, may have been lost or forgotten, I will supply this monk who preaches the Law with all these well-spoken words and letters. And I will bestow on him a dhāraṇī for the sake of preventing the loss of its memory, so that this excellent Suvarṇabhāsa, king of sūtras, may long go forth in Jambudvīpa for the welfare of those beings who have planted merit-roots under thousands of Buddhas, (so that) it may not soon disappear, (so that) numerous beings having heard this excellent Suvarṇabhāsa, king of sūtras, may have inconceivable, acute wisdom, (so that) they may obtain an inconceivable heap of knowledge, (so that) they may obtain old age and prosperity in this life, (so that) they may gain help for living and an unlimited heap of merit, [(so that) they may become skilled in various expedients,[(82)]] (so that) they may become learned in all the textbooks, (so that) they may obtain success in the performance of various arts."

(**104**) "I will explain the act of bathing attended by spells and medicaments. For the sake of the monk who preaches the Law and for the sake of those beings who listen to the Law, all the oppressions caused by planets, asterisms, birth or death, the oppressions caused by strife, quarrels, foul tumults and disorders, evil dreams, (or the god) Vināyaka, all Kākhordas and Vetālas will be completely removed."

"Medicaments[(83)] and spells with which the learned bathe: (1) *vacā*,

[(82)] Reconstructed from the Tibetan by Nobel, who (rightly) preferred *nānopāyāṃś ca prajānīyuḥ* (*Tib.* p.79 n.26).

[(83)] Not all of the thirty medicinal substances listed here can be certainly identified, and I have accordingly left them untranslated. The following brief notes concerning some of the less obscure items may give the reader an idea of the nature of the substances involved. (1) *vacā* 'sweet flag' Acorus calamus Linn. (3) *spṛkkā* Trigonella corniculata Linn. (4) *śirīṣa* 'siris tree' Albizzia Lebbek Benth. (6) *śamī* Acacia sundra DC. (10) *agaru* 'aloe' Aquilaria agallocha Roxb. (11) *tvac* 'cinnamon bark' Cinnamomum zeylanicum Nees. (12) *śrīveṣṭaka* resin of Indian olibanum (13)

(2) *gorocanā*, (3) *spṛkkā* **(105)**, (4) *śirīṣa*, (5) *śāmyaka*, (6) *śamī*, (7) *indrahastā*, (8) *mahābhāgā*, (9) *jñāmaka*, (10) *agaru*, (11) *tvac*, (12) *śrīveṣṭaka*, (13) resin of *sarja*, (14) *śallakī*, (15) *guggulu*, (16) *tagara*, (17) *patra*, (18) *śaileya*, (19) *candana*, (20) *manaḥśilā*, (21) *sarocanā*, (22) *kuṣṭha*, (23) *kuṅkuma*, (24) *musta*, (25) *sarṣapa*, (26) *nalada*, (27) *cavya*, (28) *sūkṣmailā*, (29) *uśīra*, (30) *nāgakesara*–one should pound those, when Puṣya is the asterism, into equal portions and one should consecrate the powder a hundred times with the following spell, so: *sukṛte kṛta kamalijanakarate, haṃkarāte, indrajāli, śakaddrepaśaddre, abartaksike, na kutraku, kapila kapilamati, śīlamati, sandhi dhudhumamabati, śiri śiri, satyasthite.* Hail!"

"Having made a magic circle with cow-dung, one should strew loose flowers and one should place honey in a gold vessel and in a silver vessel. **(106)** One should put there four men clad in armour and place four beautifully-adorned maidens bearing pots. One must continually scatter incense of Indian bdellium, play the five kinds of musical instruments and thoroughly adorn the goddess with umbrellas, flags, and banners. At intervals(84) one must place mirrors, arrows, and spears. Then one must make one's boundary-line. Next one must begin what has to be done. One must begin (to make) one's boundary-line in the course of uttering this spell, so: *arake, nayane, hile mile, gile, khikhile.* Hail!"

"After one has bathed behind (an image of) the Lord, one should assure peace for the bathing by uttering the following spell, so: *sagaṭe, bigaṭe, bigaṭābati.* Hail!"

sarja 'sal' Shorea robusta Gaertn. f. (14) *śallakī* 'Indian olibanum' Boswellia serrata Roxb. ex Colebr. (15) *guggulu* 'Indian bdellium' Commiphora mukul Engl. (16) *tagara* 'Indian valerian' Ervatamia divaricata Burkill. (17) *patra* 'cinnamon tree leaves' Cinnamomum tamala T. Nees et Eberm. (18) *śaileya* 'lichen' Parmelia perlata Ach. (19) *candana* 'sandal' Santalum album Linn. (20) *manaḥśilā* realgar (22) *kuṣṭha* 'costus' Saussurea lappa C.B. Clarke. (23) *kuṅkuma* 'saffron' Crocus sativus Linn. (24) *musta* 'nut grass' Cyperus rotundus Linn. (25) *sarṣapa* 'white mustard' Brassica campestris Linn. (26) *nalada* 'nard' Nardostachys jatamansi DC. (27) *cavya* 'long pepper' Piper chaba Hunter. (28) *sūkṣmailā* 'small cardamom' Elettaria cardamomum Maton. (29) *uśīra* 'vetiver' Vetiveria zizanioides (Linn.) Nash. (30) *nāgakesara* 'nagkassar' Mesua ferrea Linn.

(84) 'at intervals' renders the Tibetan *bar-bar-dag-tu*, cf. Nobel *Festschrift Schubring*, p.138. Sanskrit *padādyaś* is obscure.

"May the asterisms in the four directions protect one's life. May the oppressions caused by asterisms or birth be removed, the onset of fears caused by heaps of acts, cruel fears produced by the confusion of the elements."

"*śame, biśame.* Hail! *sagaṭe bigaṭe.* Hail! *sukhatinate.* Hail! *sāgarasaṃbhūtāya.* Hail! *skandamātrāya.* Hail! *nīlakaṇṭhāya.* Hail! **(107)** *aparājitabīryāya.* Hail! *himabatasaṃbhūtāya.* Hail! *animila-baktrāya.* Hail! *namo bhagabate brahmaṇe, namaḥ sarasvatyai debyai.* May my magic words succeed. *taṃ brahmānumanyatu.* Hail!"

"At that act of bathing, for the sake of the monk who preaches the Law, for the sake of those who listen to the Law and of those who write it down, I myself will go there. Together with the whole multitude of gods, I will cause the removal of every disease in that village, city, district, or dwelling. I will remove all oppressions caused by planets, quarrels, strife, asterisms, and birth, oppressions caused by evil dreams or (the god) Vināyaka, all Kākhordas and Vetālas, so that there may be help for living for those monks, nuns, laymen or laywomen who hold the chief sūtras, (that) they may obtain escape[(85)] from the cycle of existence and may become non-returners in supreme and perfect enlightenment, (that) they may quickly awaken before supreme and perfect enlightenment."

Then indeed the Lord offered congratulations to the goddess Sarasvatī:

"Bravo! bravo! great goddess Saravatī! You have come for the welfare of many men, for the blessing of many men, since you have spoken such words concerning spells and medicaments."**(108)**

And the goddess Sarasvatī did worship at the Lord's feet and sat down on one side.

Then indeed the teacher and expounder Kauṇḍinya, the brahmin, called to the goddess Sarasvatī:

"Sarasvatī, the great goddess, is worthy of worship, possesses great asceticism, famous in all worlds, a giver of boons, of great virtues. Dwelling on a peak, beautiful, clad in a grass garment, wearing grass clothing, she stands on one foot. All the gods assembled and spoke these words to her: 'Let loose your tongue. Speak to beings a fine

[(85)] Read *-niryāṇaṃ* for *-nirvāṇaṃ* Nobel, Berichtigungen.

speech.'"

"So be it: *mure, cire, abaje, abajabati, hiṅgule, piṅgalabati, maṅguṣe, marīci, samati, daśamati, agrīmagrī,* **(109)** *tara, citara, cabati, ciciri, śiri miri, marīci, praṇaye, lokajyeṣṭhe, lokaśreṣṭhe, lokapriye, siddihiprite, bhīmamukhi śuci khari, apratihate, apratihatabuddhi, namuci namuci mahādebi pratigṛhṇa namaskāraṃ.* May my insight be unobstructed. May my knowledge prosper in such as textbooks, verses, magic books, doctrinal books, poems. So be it: *mahāprabhāve hili hili, mili mili.* May it go forth for me by the power of the blessed goddess Sarasvatī. *karaṭe keyūre, keyūrabati, hili mili, hili mili, hili hili.* I invoke the great goddess by the truth of the Buddha, by the truth of the Law, by the truth of the Assembly, by the truth of Indra, by the truth of Varuṇa. Whatever truth-speakers there are in the world, by the truth-speaking of those truth-speakers I invoke the great goddess, so: *hili hili, hili mili hili mili.* May it go forth for me. Homage to the blessed great goddess Sarasvatī. May the words of my spell succeed. Hail!"

(110) Then the teacher and expounder Kauṇḍinya, the brahmin, praised Sarasvatī, the great goddess, in these verses:

"May all the hordes of Bhūtas hear me. I will praise the goddess, whose face is supremely, extremely beautiful, who among women in the world of gods, Gandharvas, and lords of Asuras, is the supreme, chief, excellent goddess. Sarasvatī by name has members that have piles of adornments of various virtues. Her eyes are broad. She is brilliant in merit. She is full of the virtues of pure knowledge. She is beautiful like a variety of jewels. I will praise her by reason of her distinguished virtues of excellent speech, because she causes excellent, supreme success, because of her famous teaching, because she is a mine of virtues, because she is pure and supreme, because she is brilliant as a lotus, **(111)** because her eyes are fair and excellent, because her residence is beautiful, because her appearance is beautiful, because she is thoroughly adorned with inconceivable virtues, because she resembles the moon, because her splendour is pure, because she is a mine of knowledge, because of the superiority of her mindfulness, because she is the best of lionesses, because she is a vehicle for men, because she is adorned with eight arms,[86] because her appearance is like that of the full moon, because of her heartening speech, because of her soft voice, because she is endowed with profound wisdom, because she causes the accomplishment of the best deeds, because she is an excellent being, because she is honoured by the lords of gods and Asuras, because she is praised in all the dwellings of a multitude of gods and Asuras, because she is continually worshipped in the abode of a multitude of Bhūtas. Hail!"

"I bow down to this goddess. May she give me a special mass of virtues. May she grant me success in every act. May she continually protect me in the midst of enemies." **(112)**

(If) one rises up in the morning, and, pure, utters these complete syllables and full words, one obtains all desires, wealth and grain, and one gains splendid, noble success.

So (ends) the seventh chapter, the Chapter on Sarasvatī, in the excellent Suvarṇabhāsa, king of sūtras.

8. Chapter on Śri

Then indeed the great goddess Śrī spoke thus to the Lord:

"I, dear Lord, the great goddess Śrī, will give zeal to that monk who preaches the Law as well as such equipment as garments, begging-bowl, bed, seat, and medicines to deal with illness, and other excellent equipment, so that the **(113)** preacher of the Law may be provided with every equipment, and he may have no lack, he may be sound in mind, he may pass night and day with happy mind, he may take up from this excellent Suvarṇabhāsa, king of sūtras, various words and letters, he may examine them, so that, for the welfare of those beings who have planted merit-roots under thousands of Buddhas, this excellent Suvarṇabhāsa, king of sūtras, may long go forth in Jambudvīpa, may not quickly disappear, and beings may hear the excellent Suvarṇabhāsa, king of sūtras, and may during numerous hundreds of thousands of millions of aeons experience inconceivable divine and human pleasures, that famine may disappear, and plenty may be

[86] This is thought to be the source of the eight-armed representation of Sarasvatī in Japanese iconography. See *Hôbôgirin* s.v. *Benzaiten*.

manifest, that beings may be blessed with the supply of human blessings, may meet Tathāgatas, and in future time may awaken to supreme and perfect enlightenment, that all the woes of hells, animals, and the world of Yama, may be fully cut off."

There (was) a Tathāgata, Arhat, fully enlightened one, named Ratnakusumaguṇasāgaravaiḍūryakanakagirisuvarṇakāñcanaprabhāsaśrī, where the great goddess Śrī **(114)** planted a merit-root. Where *she[87] now watches over any direction, surveys any direction, approaches any direction, in that direction numerous hundreds of thousands of millions of beings will be blessed with the supply of every blessing, will have no deficiency. Those beings will be replete with every equipment, with food, drink, wealth, grain, gold, jewels, pearls, beryl, conches, **(115)** crystal, coral, gold, silver, and other items. By the power of the great goddess Śrī, homage must be done to that Tathāgata. Perfumes, flowers, and incense must be offered. One must thrice utter the name of the great goddess Śrī. One must offer her perfumes, flowers, and incense. One must walk around scattering juices.[88] For him there will grow a great heap of corn. There this is to be said: "The earth's savour grows in the earth. The deities rejoice continually. The deities of the fruits, crops, shrubs, bushes, and trees make the crops grow in brilliant condition."

The name of the excellent Suvarṇabhāsa, king of sūtras, must be uttered. Those beings the great goddess Śrī will watch over. For them she will create great good fortune. **(116)**

The great goddess Śrī was dwelling in the palace Aḍakāvatī in the excellent park Puṇyakusumaprabhā in the abode[89] named Suvarṇa-

[87] Sanskrit has only *sa* 'he', which is unclear here. According to Nobel, Sanskrit text, p.114 n.4 *sa* can only be understood as referring to the *dharmabhāṇaka* mentioned at the beginning of the chapter. However, as R. Tsuchida has pointed out in *CAJ*, 29, 1985, 128-133 the context requires the subject to be the goddess Śrī. This would in effect mean that the MS. reading *sa* is a mistake for *sā*.

[88] The reading of MSS. ABCDEJ *rasa-vihārāṇi* should be retained as pointed out by Skjærvø, although its precise interpretation is not clear. The Khotanese version has *raysa vara viśtāña* 'juices are to be placed there' and the Tibetan *ro sna-ćhogs kyaṅ byin* 'and various juices are to be offered'.

[89] For Nobel's *bhavanavare* reconstructed from the Tibetan read *bhavane* as indicated by MSS. CF.

dhvaja made of the seven jewels. Whatever man should be desirous of increasing his heap of corn, he should thoroughly purify his house, bathe well, clothe himself in pure, white garments and wear well-perfumed clothing. Doing homage, he should thrice utter the name of the Lord Ratnakusumaguṇasāgaravaiḍūryakanakagirisuvarṇakāñcana-prabhāsaśrī, the Tathāgata, Arhat, fully enlightened one. With the help of the great goddess Śrī worship is to be done to that Tathāgata. Flowers, incense, and perfumes must be offered. One must walk around scattering various juices.[90] One must thrice utter the name of the excellent Suvarṇabhāsa, king of sūtras. The word of truth must be spoken. Homage must be done to the great goddess Śrī. Flowers and incense must be offered. One must walk around scattering various juices. By the power of this excellent Suvarṇabhāsa, **(117)** king of sūtras, at that time the great goddess Śrī will watch over that house. And she will make increase the great heap of his corn. One who desires to invoke the great goddess Śrī must recollect the following magic spells: "Homage to all the Buddhas, past, future, and present. Homage to all the Buddhas and Bodhisattvas. Homage to the Bodhisattvas beginning with Maitreya." When homage has been done to those, I employ the following magic spell.[91] May this magic spell[92] succeed for me. So be it: *pratipūrṇapāre, samantadarśane, mahābihāragate, samantabedanagate, mahākāryapratiprāpaṇe, sattva-arthasamantānuprapure, āyānadharmatā mahābhogine, mahāmaitri-upasaṃhite, hitaiṣi, saṃgrihīte, tesamarthānupālani.*

These are the magic words for lawful consecration of the head, the words for complete[93] success, the words whose meaning cannot deceive. [94](As for) one who in the midst of beings pursues his career with blameless merit-roots, uttering and maintaining (the magic

[90] Reading *nānā-rasa-vihārāś* (Skjærvø) on p. 116 lines 9 and 12 as on p. 115 line 5 above.

[91] Read *imāṃ vidyāṃ* as MSS. CJ for Nobel's *imā vidyāḥ*.

[92] Read *iyaṃ me vidyā samṛdhyatu* as indicated by the MSS. as well as the Tibetan and Khotanese versions.

[93] The Sanskrit MSS. seem to indicate a reading **ekāṃśasiddhipadā*, cf. R. Tsuchida, *CAJ*, 29, 1985, 133. The Khotanese *īyāndu pätālye* (54r7 *KT* 1.238) 'constantly successes' is apparently not literal.

[94] The precise reading and interpretation of this sentence remains obscure.

spells) (**118**) for seven years, observing the sabbaths by keeping the eight moral precepts, having done worship morning and evening to all the Lord Buddhas with flowers, perfumes, and incense, in order to fulfill the omniscience of himself and of all beings, may all his wishes succeed, may they quickly succeed. Having made his house pure or his monastery or forest retreat, and having made a circle of cow-dung, he must offer perfumes, flowers, and incense. He must provide a pure seat. He must go to (a place) bestrewn with flowers. Then at that moment the great goddess Śrī will enter and stay there. Thereafter in that house, village, city, (**119**) settlement, monastery or forest retreat, no one at all will cause deficiency. They will be replete with all equipment, gold, jewel, wealth or grain, blessed with the supply of every blessing. Whatever merit-roots are performed, the great goddess Śrī must be given the chief share of them all. As long as he lives, she will remain there. She will not hesitate, and all their desires will be fulfilled.(95)

So (ends) the eighth chapter, the Chapter on Śrī, the great goddess, in the excellent Suvarṇabhāsa, king of sūtras.

9. Chapter on the Maintenance of the Names of Buddhas and Bodhisattvas(96)

Homage to the Lord Ratnaśikhin, the Tathāgata. [Homage to the Tathāgata Vimalojjvalaratnaraśmiprabhāsaketu. Homage to the Tathāgata Suvarṇajaṃbudhvajakāñcanābha. Homage to the Tathāgata *Suvarṇabhāsagarbha. Homage to the Tathāgata Suvarṇaśataraśmiprabhāsaketu.](97) Homage to the Tathāgata Suvarṇaratnākaracchatrakūṭa.

(95) Read *sarvābhiprāyāś...paripūrayiṣyantīti* Nobel, *Tib.* p.91 n.129.

(96) Not originally a separate chapter but the beginning of chapter 10 as in Tib. (see Nobel, Sanskrit text, p.xxxiii) and in Khotanese (*KT* 1.239).

(97) Reconstructed by Nobel from Tibetan. Nobel reconstructed *Vimalojjvalaratnasuvarṇabhāsaketu for Tibetan dri-ma med-par hbar-ba rin-chen gser-gyi hod-zer snaṅ-bahi tog, but the Khotanese version has Vimalojvalaratnaraśmiprrabhāsakettu, which indicates Sanskrit Vimalojjvalaratnaraśmiprabhāsaketu. For Tibetan hjam-buhi gser-gyi rgyal-mćhan gser-du snaṅ-ba Nobel reconstructed *Jambusuvarṇadhvajakāñcanabhāsa, but the Khotanese has Suvarṇajaṃbudvajakāṃcanābhu, which indicates Sanskrit Suvarṇajaṃbudhvajakāñcanābha. For

(**120**) Homage to the Tathāgata Suvarṇapuṣpojjvalaraśmiketu. Homage to the Tathāgata Mahāpradīpa. Homage to the Tathāgata Ratnaketu. The Bodhisattva named Ruciraketu, the Bodhisattva named Suvarṇabhāsottama, the Bodhisattva named Suvarṇagarbha, the Bodhisattva named Sadāprarudita, the Bodhisattva named Dharmodgata, in the east the Tathāgata named Akṣobhya, in the south the Tathāgata named Ratnaketu, in the west the Tathāgata named Amitāyus, in the north the Tathāgata named Dundubhisvara–whoever holds, recites, explains these Tathāgata-names (and) Bodhisattva-names in the excellent Suvarṇabhāsa, king of sūtras, he will always be mindful of his births.

So (ends) the ninth chapter, the Chapter on the Maintenance of the Names of Buddhas and Bodhisattvas. (**121**)

10. Chapter on Dṛḍhā

Then indeed the earth-goddess Dṛḍhā spoke thus to the Lord:

"In whatever village, city, settlement, district, forest-region, mountain-cavern or royal palace this excellent Suvarṇabhāsa, king of sūtras, dear Lord, now and in future time shall go forth, I, dear Lord, the earth-goddess Dṛḍhā will approach that village, city, settlement, district, forest-region, mountain-cavern or royal palace. Wherever this excellent Suvarṇabhāsa, king of sūtras, shall be expounded in detail, in whichever region of the earth, Lord, the seat of the Law will have been provided for the monk who preaches the Law, wherever the preacher of the Law, having sat on that seat, shall expound in detail this excellent Suvarṇabhāsa, king of sūtras, there I, dear Lord, the earth-goddess Dṛḍhā, will come to those regions of the earth. Having gone up to the seat of the Law with my invisible body I will lean with my head upon the soles of the feet of the monk who is preaching the Law. And I will satisfy myself with that hearing of the Law, (**122**)

Tibetan gser-du snaṅ-bahi sñiṅ-po Nobel reconstructed *Suvarṇabhāsagarbha. This name is not represented in the Khotanese version. For Tibetan ñi-ma brgyahi hod-zer snaṅ-bahi sñiṅ-po Nobel reconstructed Suvarṇaśataraśmibhāsagarbha, but the Khotanese has Svarṇaśataraśmiprabhāsakettu, which indicates Sanskrit Suvarṇa-śataraśmiprabhāsaketu.

with the nectar juice of the Law. I will do homage, I will rejoice. When I have satisfied myself, done homage, rejoiced, I will cause to increase in respect of the savour of the earth a mass of earth six million eight hundred[98] thousand leagues in extent as far as the foundation of the earth made of the thunderbolt. I will do homage, I will completely fill it. And above it I will make moist with the moist savour of the earth this circle of the earth that reaches the edge of the ocean. And I will make this great earth stronger so that in this Jambu-dvīpa the various grasses, bushes, plants, and trees will grow stronger. All the trees in parks and groves and all the various leaves, flowers, fruits, and crops will be stronger, will be more fragrant, more moist, more tasty, will be more beautiful, greater. And when those beings have enjoyed those various drinks and foods, they will increase their longevity, strength, complexion, and senses. And having become endowed with brilliance, power, complexion, and form, they will perform the various numerous hundreds of thousands of activities on the earth. They will be devoted. They will be thorough. **(123)** They will do acts that have to be done with power. For this reason, dear Lord, the whole of Jambudvīpa will become peaceful, will become plentiful, flourishing, delightful, and full of many people and men. And in the whole of Jambudvīpa all beings will be blessed, will experience a variety of pleasure. Those beings will be endowed with brilliance, power, complexion, and form. For the sake of this excellent Suvarṇabhāsa, king of sūtras, they will approach the presence of those monks, nuns, laymen and laywomen who hold the chief sūtras, preachers of the Law[99] upon the seats of the Law. Having approached, with their minds pure, those beings[100] will beseech those preachers of the Law, for the good, welfare, and blessing of all beings, to expound this excellent Suvarṇabhāsa, king of sūtras. Why is that? When, dear Lord, this excellent Suvarṇabhāsa, king of sūtras, is being

[98] Reading with MS. G °*śatasahasraṃ* Nobel, *Tib.* p.93 n.54 and Chinese p.273 n.3.

[99] Read *dharmabhāṇakānāṃ* with MS. G corresponding to Khotanese *dāta-hvāñānu*.

[100] Read *tāni sattvāni* with MS. G, which corresponds to Khotanese *ttä uysnaura*.

expounded, I, the earth-goddess Dṛḍhā, together with my retinue, will become stronger and more powerful. In our body there will be produced great power, fortitude, and strength. Brilliance, glory and fortune will enter our body. When I, dear Lord, the earth-goddess Dṛḍhā, have been satisfied with the nectar juice of the Law (**124**) and have obtained great brilliance, fortitude, strength, and force, this Jambudvīpa with its seven thousand leagues[101] of the great earth will increase in the savour of its earth. And the great earth will become stronger. And, dear Lord, all those beings who are dependent upon the earth will find increase, extension, and expansion. And they will become great. And having become great, those beings will enjoy the various enjoyments and pleasures on earth and will experience blessings. And may they enjoy all the various foods, drinks, nourishment, clothes, beds, seats, dwellings, residences, palaces, parks, rivers, ponds, springs, lakes, pools, and tanks, these and similar varieties of aids and blessings existing on the earth, manifest on the earth and dependent upon the earth. For this reason, dear Lord, all beings should show gratitude to us. Assuredly this excellent Suvarṇabhāsa, king of sūtras, must be listened to respectfully, be respected, honoured, revered, worshipped. And when, dear Lord, all those beings come out of their various residences, their various houses, to approach those preachers of the Law, having approached, (**125**) may they listen to this excellent Suvarṇabhāsa, king of sūtras. And, moreover, having listened, when they have severally entered their various residences, houses, villages, cities or settlements, when they have gone to their own homes, may they converse thus with one another: 'Today we have heard the profound Law. Today we have gained an inconceivable heap of merit. [By this hearing of the Law we

[101] Read *°sāhasriko 'yaṃ* with MS. J (Skjærvø). With a Sanskrit adjective the Tibetan genitive is compatible. Jambudvīpa is traditionally said to be 7.000 leagues in extent in Buddhist cosmography. See W. Kirfel, *Die Kosmographie der Inder,* Bonn and Leipzig 1920 (repr. Hildesheim 1967), p.188, citing Lalitavistara (ed. S. Lefmann) p.149 (*jambudvīpaḥ saptayojanasahasrāṇi*). For the tradition in Khotanese, see R.E. Emmerick, *JRAS,* 1967, 22-25. It occurs also in the Khotanese Sudhana story, see H.W. Bailey, *BSOAS,* XXIX.3, 1966, 511.

have pleased[(102)] numerous hundreds of thousands of Tathāgatas.[(103)]] By this hearing of the Law [we have today[(104)]] escaped from hell, have escaped from the region of animals, of the world of Yama, and of ghosts. Today by this hearing of the Law we will have gained rebirth among gods and men in future[(105)] time during numerous hundreds of thousands of births'. And when they have returned to their various homes, may they tell other beings even a single illustration from this excellent Suvarṇabhāsa, king of sūtras; may they cause other beings to hear from this excellent Suvarṇabhāsa, king of sūtras, even a single chapter or a single birth-story [or even the name of a single Bodhisattva or the name of a single Tathāgata,[(106)]] even a four-verse stanza, even a single verse; **(126)** may they cause other beings to hear even the mere name of this excellent Suvarṇabhāsa, king of sūtras. Wherever, dear Lord, the various beings in various regions of the earth tell one another these and similar varieties of sūtra-arguments or cause them to be heard or should talk about them, all those regions of the earth, dear Lord, will become stronger and will become more moist. For all the beings in those regions of the earth, the various savours of the earth, all its aids, will become more abundant, will increase, will expand. All those beings will be blessed. They will have great wealth and great enjoyment but will be devoted to liberality. They will have faith in the Three Jewels."

When this had been said, the Lord spoke thus to the earth-goddess Dṛḍhā:

"Whatever beings, earth-goddess, may hear even a single verse from this excellent Suvarṇabhāsa, king of sūtras, they will transmigrate from this world of men and will be reborn among the group

[(102)] Nobel later preferred to reconstruct *ārāgitāni* rather than *ārādhitāni* Nobel, Berichtigungen. The Khotanese has *ārāhäta hämāre*.

[(103)] This sentence has been reconstructed by Nobel from the Tibetan, with which the Khotanese agrees closely.

[(104)] Nobel reconstructed *adya vayaṃ* from the Tibetan version. The Khotanese has the exactly corresponding *īmu muhu*.

[(105)] Read *dharmaśravaṇenānāgate* with *°ānāgate* following Tibetan *ma-hoṅs-pahi*. Nobel's *dharmaśravaṇenāgate* appears to be merely a misprint.

[(106)] Reconstructed by Nobel from the Tibetan. The Khotanese corresponds exactly.

of Thirty-three gods (and) among other groups of gods. Whatever beings, earth-goddess, adorn those places for this excellent Suvarṇabhāsa, king of sūtras, cover them with even a single umbrella, a single flag, or a single piece of cloth, those adorned places, earth-goddess, (**127**) will become divine palaces, made of the seven jewels, adorned with every adornment, among the group of seven[(107)] gods dwelling in the realm of desire. And when those beings transmigrate from this world of men, they will be reborn in those divine palaces made of the seven jewels. They will be reborn, earth-goddess, seven times in each divine palace made of the seven jewels. They will experience inconceivable divine blessings."

When this had been said, the earth-goddess Dṛḍhā spoke thus to the Lord:

"Therefore, dear Lord, I, the earth-goddess Dṛḍhā, will dwell in those regions of the earth, where the monk who preaches the Law has sat upon the seat of the Law. With invisible body I will lean my head upon the soles of the feet of that monk who preaches the Law, so that this excellent Suvarṇabhāsa, king of sūtras, may, for the welfare of those beings who have planted merit-roots under thousands of Buddhas, long go forth in Jambudvīpa and not quickly disappear. And may beings hear this excellent Suvarṇabhāsa, king of sūtras. May they in future time during numerous hundreds of thousands of millions of aeons experience inconceivable divine and human pleasures. May they meet Tathāgatas. In future time may they awaken to supreme and perfect enlightenment and may all the woes of hells, animalhood, and the world of Yama be wholly cut off." (**128**)

So (ends) the tenth chapter, the Chapter on the Earth-goddess Dṛḍhā, in the excellent Suvarṇabhāsa, king of sūtras.

11. Chapter on Saṃjñāya

Then indeed the great general of the Yakṣas called Saṃjñāya, together with twenty-eight great Yakṣa generals, rose up from his

(107) The *kāmāvacara*-gods are usually six as in I-tsing (p.276 n.4). The number 'seven' (also in Tib. I) may have been induced by the *saptavārān* 'seven times' immediately below.

seat, covered one shoulder with his robe, placed his right knee on the ground, made the gesture of reverence in the direction of the Lord and spoke thus to the Lord:

"In whatever village, city, settlement, district, forest-region, mountain-cavern or royal palace, this, dear Lord, excellent Suvarṇabhāsa, king of sūtras, shall go forth in this and in future time, there I, dear Lord, the great Yakṣa general called Saṃjñāya, together with the twenty-eight great Yakṣa generals, will approach that village, city, settlement, district, forest-region, mountain-cavern or royal palace. With invisible body I will give protection to the monk who preaches the Law, I will give deliverance, help, defence, escape from punishment, peace, and welfare. To all those (**129**) women, men, boys, and girls who hear the Law, whoever should hear even one four-verse stanza, even one verse, from this excellent Suvarṇabhāsa, king of sūtras, should hear even only the name of a single Bodhisattva from this excellent Suvarṇabhāsa, king of sūtras, should accept it, should hear the name of a single Tathāgata, even the name of this excellent Suvarṇabhāsa, king of sūtras, should accept it–to all those I will give protection, I will give aid, defence, deliverance, escape from punishment, peace, and welfare. And to their dwellings, their houses, their villages, their cities, their settlements, their forests, and their palaces I will give protection, I will give deliverance, aid, defence, escape from punishment, peace, and welfare."

"For what reason, [dear Lord, have I been given the name Saṃjñāya, the great Yakṣa general? ... By me, dear Lord, are all things known,[(108)]] all things are fully known, all things are perceived. However many are all things, how all things are, what things exist, of what kinds are all things, (**130**) all things, dear Lord, are apparent to me. Inconceivable, dear Lord, is the splendour of my knowledge, inconceivable the clarity of my knowledge, inconceivable the extent of my knowledge, inconceivable the quantity of my knowledge. Inconceivable, dear Lord, is the sphere of my knowledge, which operates among all things. And as, dear Lord, all things are fully known by me,

[(108)] Reconstructed by Nobel from Tibetan. He later preferred to reconstruct *saṃjñodapādi* (Nobel, *Tib.* p.101 n.43). The somewhat fragmentary Khotanese version of this passage confirms the meaning indicated.

fully examined, fully comprehended, fully surveyed, fully perceived, for this reason, dear Lord, I, Saṃjñāya, the great general of the Yakṣas, have been given[(109)] the name Saṃjñāya."

"I, dear Lord, in order to adorn the speech of the monk who preaches the Law, will contribute eloquence. I will insert strength into his hair-pores. I will produce in his body great energy, strength, and prowess. I will make inconceivable the splendour of his knowledge. I will make him perceive his mindfulness. I will give him great zeal, so that the preacher of the Law may not be weary in body, that his body may have happy senses, that he may be full of joy, so that this excellent Suvarṇabhāsa, king of sūtras, for the welfare of those beings who have planted merit-roots under thousands of Buddhas, may long go forth in Jambudvīpa, may not quickly disappear, (so that) beings may hear this excellent Suvarṇabhāsa, king of sūtras, (so that) they may obtain an inconceivable (**131**) quantity of knowledge, they may become wise, they may gain an unlimited mass of merit, they may in future time during numerous hundreds of thousands of millions of aeons experience inconceivable divine and human pleasures, they may meet Tathāgatas, they may in future time awaken to supreme and perfect enlightenment and all the woes of hell, animalhood, and the world of Yama may be wholly cut off."

So (ends) the eleventh chapter, the Chapter on Saṃjñāya, in the excellent Suvarṇabhāsa, king of sūtras.

12. Chapter on Instruction concerning Divine Kings

Homage to the Lord Ratnakusumaguṇasāgaravaiḍūryakanakagiri-suvarṇakāñcanaprabhāsaśrī, the Tathāgata. Arhat, fully enlightened one. Homage to the Tathāgata Śākyamuni, whose body is adorned with numerous hundreds of thousands of millions of virtues and who has made[(110)] shine the lamp of his Law. Homage to (**132**) the great goddess Śrī, who is endowed with unlimited virtues, grain, and blessings. Homage to the great goddess Sarasvatī, who is equipped with

(109) Read *saṃjñodapādi* for *nāmadheyaṃ samudapādi* Nobel, *Tib.* p.101 n.42.

(110) Read *jvālitā* for *jvalati* Nobel, *Tib.* p.103 n.4, as indicated by MS. G and the Tibetan.

unlimited wisdom and virtues.

Then indeed at that time at that moment, King Balendraketu spoke thus to his son King Ruciraketu, whom he had not long ago consecrated and who was established in his new royalty:

"There is, son, a textbook for kings called *Instruction concerning Divine Kings*, which formerly, when I had just been consecrated and established in new royalty I received in the presence of my father King Varendraketu. I exercised sovereignty for twenty thousand years according to that royal textbook *Instruction concerning Divine Kings*. I do not know that I ever stood[(111)] on the side of anyone unlawfully even if only for the measure of a single moment's thought. What then, son, is that textbook for kings called *Instruction concerning Divine Kings*?"

Then indeed, noble deity, King Balendraketu at that time, at that moment, expounded in detail to his son King Ruciraketu in these verses the textbook for kings called *Instruction concerning Divine Kings*. **(133)**

"I will set forth the textbook for kings, which causes the welfare of all beings, disposes of all doubts, and removes all evil deeds. May all kings here severally be joyful-minded. May you listen to the whole *Instruction concerning Divine Kings* with your hands in the gesture of reverence."

"On this lord of mountains Vajrākara at a meeting of the divine kings, there arose a questioning[(112)] of King Brahma by the world-protectors: 'You, Brahma, are a venerable teacher among the gods, you are lord of the gods. Solve our problems. Remove our doubt. Why is a king, though born among men, called "divine"? And for what reason is a king called a "divine son"? If he is born here in the world of men, he should become king, but how will a god exercise kingship among men?'" **(134)**

"Thus then was King Brahma interrogated by the world-protectors.

[(111)] Read *sthitapūrvaḥ* (cf. MS. G) as suggested by R. Tsuchida, *CAJ*, 29, 1985, 134.

[(112)] Reading *°paripṛcchatā* with MS. G, as proposed by F. Edgerton, *Buddhist Hybrid Sanskrit Grammar and Dictionary*, vol.2: *Dictionary*, New Haven 1953, s.v. *paripṛccha-tā*.

The venerable teacher of the gods[(113)] Brahma spoke thus to the world-protectors: 'If now I have been so interrogated by the world-protectors, I will now, for the good and welfare of all beings, speak of this excellent teaching. I will speak of the origin of kings, (their) arising[(114)] in the abode of men, and for what reason they become kings in their territories. Under the blessing of the divine kings, he will enter the womb of his mother. Having first been blessed by the gods, he afterwards enters her womb. Although as king he is born and dies in the world of men, (**135**) yet since he comes from the gods he is called a divine son. The Thirty-three divine kings have given a portion to the king (saying) "You (are our) son,[(115)] a lord of men magically created by[(116)] all the gods". For the sake of suppressing what is unlawful, a destroyer of evil deeds, he would establish beings in good activity in order to send them to the abode of the gods. (**136**) Whether the lord of men (is) a man or a god, a Gandharva, a Rākṣasa, an untouchable, he removes evil deeds. The king is the parent of those who do good deeds. The king has been blessed by the gods as one who exhibits[(117)] (their) fruition and fruit. The king has been blessed by the gods as belonging to the present world to show the fruition and fruit of deeds well done and of deeds ill done. For when a king overlooks an evil deed in his territory and does not inflict appropriate punishment on the evil person, in the neglect of evil deeds lawlessness grows greatly, wicked acts and quarrels arise in great number in the realm. The chief gods are wrathful in the dwellings of the Thirty-three (**137**) when a king overlooks an evil deed in his territory. His territory is smitten with dreadful, most terrible acts of wickedness,

(113) Read *sa vai sura-gurur* with MS. J (Skjærvø), cf. Tibetan *lḫa-yi gćo-bo ... des*.

(114) Read *utpādaṃ* (Skjærvø) as indicated by MSS. CFJ and by the Khotanese version, which has *kho hämāre marata hvaṃ'duvo'* 'how they arise here among men'.

(115) Reading *putras tvaṃ* with MSS. GJ, cf. R. Tsuchida, *CAJ*, 29, 1985, 134-135.

(116) I have construed *sarvadevānāṃ* with *nirmito* following the Khotanese version, which has: *cuī biśśä gyasta närmitāndä hvąndānu hvāṣṭu rrāyse* (*KT* 5.114) 'because all the gods magically created him as chief ruler of men'.

(117) Retain *-darśī*, the reading of the MSS. ABCDE, supported by Khotanese *näjsätā'kä*.

and his realm is destroyed[118] on the arrival of a foreign army, his enjoyments and houses. Whoever has accumulated wealth, by various evil acts they deprive one another of them. If he does not perform the duty on account of which he has kingship, he destroys his own realm, just as the lord of elephants (tramples) on a lotus-pool. Unfavourable winds will blow; unfavourable showers of rain (will fall); unfavourable (will be) planets and asterisms, likewise moon and sun. Crop, flower, fruit, and seed will not ripen in due season. Famine will arise there where the king is neglectful. Unhappy in mind will the gods be in their dwellings when the king overlooks an evil deed in his territory. All the kings of the gods will say to one another: **(138)** 'Unlawful is this king, for he supports the side of the lawless.' This king will ere long anger the gods. Through the anger of the gods his territory will perish. There will be destruction by the weapon and lawlessness in that[119] territory. Wicked acts, quarrels, diseases will arise. The lords of the gods will be angry. The gods will ignore him. His realm will be ruined. The king will come to grief. He will find himself separated from his loved ones, from brother or son, separated from his beloved wife. Or his daughter will die. There will be showers of meteors, likewise mock suns. Fear of foreign armies and famine will increase greatly. **(139)** His beloved minister will die and also his beloved elephant. As soon as they have died, his beloved horses and female camels will likewise (die). They will carry off one another's house, enjoyments, wealth. In every district they will slay one another with arms. In the territories there will be disputes, quarrels, evil acts. An evil demon will enter the realm. There will be severe disease. After that the venerable will become lawless. His ministers and attendants will become lawless. After that there will be respect for the lawless person and there will be constantly oppression of law-abiding beings. Through[120] honour for lawless people and in the case of

[118] The MSS. read *vinaśyanti* as pointed out by Nobel, *Tib.* p.106 n.78.

[119] Read *viṣaye 'tra* following MSS. F and J. The Khotanese has *praharaṇyau bvānä hämäte kāmiña kṣīra adāta hämāre* 'There will be destruction by weapons there in the territory in which there are acts of lawlessness'. Khotanese *vara* may correspond to *atra* whereas *kāmiña* appears to correspond to the variant *yatra*.

[120] Read *saṃmānair dharmikāṇāṃ ca nigrahe* (Skjærvø). As Nobel pointed out, the instrumental or locative is expected as indicated by the Tibetan and Khotanese

oppression of the law-abiding, three things go wild there: asterisms, water, and winds. Three things perish when there is acceptance of lawless people: the savour, essence, and strength[(121)] of the Good Law, the strength of beings, and the savour of the earth. **(140)** (Where there is) honour for untruthful people and dishonour for truthful people, there will be there three things: famine, thunderbolt, and death (by plague).[(122)] After that there will be no savour or strength in fruit or crop. Many beings will become ill in those territories. Large sweet fruits in those territories will become small, bitter, and sharp. Play, laughter, and pleasure, things previously enjoyable, will become feeble and unenjoyable, fraught with hundreds of troubles. The savour of the moist essence of crops and fruits will disappear. Thus they will not satisfy the body, the senses, or the elements. Beings will become of bad complexion, of very little strength, and very weak. Having eaten much food they will not attain satiety. After that they will get no strength, prowess or energy. Beings in those territories will become without prowess. Beings will become disease-ridden, oppressed by various illnesses. There will arise evil demons, asterisms, and various Rākṣasas. **(141)** A king would be lawless if he stood on the side of lawlessness: the three spheres, the circle[(123)] of the whole triple world are harmed. Numerous such evils arise in those territories when a king is partisan and overlooks an evil act. (If) he overlooks[(124)] an evil act,

versions.

(121) Read *saddharma-rasa-maṇḍojaḥ* with MS. J (Skjærvø) in accord with Khotanese *rraṣṭye dātä raysä vasutättātä ūśä* 'the savour, purity, strength of the right Law'.

(122) J.W. de Jong (*IIJ*, XIV, 1972, 121) suggests that Dharmakṣema's 'epidemic' and the Tibetan rendering *hchi* 'death' may render Sanskrit *māri, mārī* or *māra* 'plague, pestilence'. Note also Khotanese *papatai āchei* '*papatai* disease' (65r2 *KT* 5.116). However, the MSS. do not support a long vowel. *malaṃ* in MSS. BDE and *mala* in MS. F may have arisen from *maraṃ* due to the preceding *nir* of *aśanir* since F actually has *sunirmmala*. The Tibetan *hchi* 'death' could be a literal rendering of Sanskrit *maraṃ*, the other versions providing an elaboration.

(123) Reading *maṇḍalaṃ* with the MSS.

(124) Nobel, Sanskrit text, p.141 n.14 suggests reading *samupekṣate* for MS. *samupekṣataḥ*, but it may be preferable to interpret *samupekṣataḥ* as nom. sg. masc. of the pres. part. with R. Tsuchida, *CAJ*, 29, 1985, 135-136. The Khotanese 3 sg. present *anaṃdīśśäte* may simply reflect the different syntax of Khotanese.

a king does not exercise his kingship according to the duty for which he was consecrated by the lords of the gods. By good action beings are reborn as gods in the abode of the gods, but by evil action they go among ghosts, animals or the hells. Because of the evil act, when a king overlooks an evil act in his territory, he makes burn[(125)] the dwellings of the Thirty-three gods. He becomes[(126)] guilty towards his forefathers (and) the kings of the gods. That is not (true) sonship nor would (true) kingship be exercised. When his realm is being destroyed by very terrible acts, therefore is the king appointed by the lords of the gods in the abode of men: for the sake of suppressing evil acts, a promoter of good acts, the king produces fruition for beings in this life. (**142**) He is called king because he acts in various ways in order to demonstrate the fruition and fruit of acts that are well done or ill done. He has been blessed by multitudes of gods and approved by deities for the sake of himself, for the sake of others, for the sake of the Law and of his territory. In order to control wicked, evil people in his realms, he should give up life and sovereignty for the sake of the Law and of his territory. He must not knowingly without examination overlook a lawless act. No other destruction in his territory is so terrible. When on the arising of evil there is no suppression of the evil-doer[(127)], (**143**) there arise in abundance very terrible evils in that territory. This realm is destroyed as a great pool by elephants, the lords of the gods are wrathful, and the abode of the gods is destroyed. All things become unfavourable for that territory. Therefore he should impose restraint on evil-doers in conformity with their crime. He should protect his realm according to the Law and he should not perform a lawless act. Even giving up his life, he should not take sides. The king should be impartial toward relatives and other people, all the people in his realm. He should not take sides. The law-abiding king fills the triple world with his fame and gladdens[(128)] the lords of

(125) Read °*bhavanān pratāpayati*: see P.O. Skjærvø, *Studies in the vocabulary of Khotanese I*, Wien 1982, 60-61.

(126) Read *bhavate* (for *bhavane*) with ACF, supported by Khotanese *hämäte* 'becomes' (66r1 *KT* 5.117).

(127) Read *śāṭhya-kartar'* (Skjærvø).

(128) Read *harṣayiṣyati* with the MSS. in accord with Khotanese *sīra padīmäte* 'he makes contented'.

the gods in the dwellings of the Thirty-three: 'In Jambudvīpa the law-abiding king is thus our son. (**144**) He rules his realm according to the Law. He establishes people in good action. And this king by good action sends people here, and he makes the abode of the gods full of gods and divine sons.' (When) he rules his realm according to the Law, the kings (of the gods) are very joyful. The lords of the gods are pleased. They protect this king. Asterisms and likewise moon and sun move properly. In due time the winds blow. In due time the god sends rain. The god provides plenty in the realm and in the abode of the gods. The abode of the gods becomes full of immortals and immortals' sons. Therefore a king should give up his own beloved life but should not give up the Jewel of the Law, by which the world may become blessed. He should keep the law-abiding company of those who are fully endowed with virtues, who are always contented with their own people and continually refrain from evil. (**145**) He should protect his realm according to the Law. He should teach the Law. He should establish beings in good action and he should restrain them from evil action.[(129)] Plenty arises in the realm (and) the king becomes famous when he imposes appropriate restraint upon evil-doers. The king becomes famous (and) easily protects his subjects.'"

So (ends) the twelfth chapter, the Chapter on Regal Science, called *Instruction concerning Divine Kings*, in the excellent Suvarṇabhāsa, king of sūtras.

13. CHAPTER ON SUSAṂBHAVA

When I became Cakravartin-king then I gave up the earth with its oceans. (**146**) I presented the four continents full of jewels to the former Buddhas. And there is no loved, pleasing object which I did nor formerly give up. For the sake of my search for the one who has the Law as his body I gave up my dear life during numerous aeons, as (I did) during inconceivable previous aeons in the Order of the Buddha Ratnaśikhin. When that Buddha had attained complete Nirvāṇa, there arose a king called Susaṃbhava. This Cakravartin, lord of

[(129)] Possibly read with MS. F *duṣkṛtena* corresponding to the Tibetan *ñes-byed-las* and the Khotanese *dīryau häryau*. Cf. R. Tsuchida, *CAJ*, 29, 1985, 136.

the four continents, rules the earth as far as the ocean. (**147**) And then the excellent king was asleep in the Jinendraghoṣā palace. Hearing in his dream the virtues of the Buddha, he saw Ratnoccaya, a preacher of the Law, shining in the midst of the sun, expounding this king of sūtras. (**148**) And the king woke from his sleep. His whole body was full of happiness. Going joyfully out of his palace, he approached the excellent assembly of the disciples. He did homage to the Buddha's disciples. He asked after Ratnoccaya, the preacher of the Law: "Where in this noble assembly is the monk called Ratnoccaya, who is endowed with virtues?" Then Ratnoccaya was elsewhere, sitting in a cave, reflecting on this king of sūtras, studying it, seated comfortably. Then they showed the king the monk Ratnoccaya, the preacher of the Good Law, (**149**) sitting elsewhere in a cave, refulgent with brilliance, splendour, and glory. Here this Ratnoccaya, the preacher of the Law, maintained the profound sphere of activity of the Buddha. He continually proclaimed the king of sūtras called the excellent Suvarṇabhāsa. Worshipping the feet of Ratnoccaya, King Susaṃbhava said this: "Expound to me, you whose face resembles the full moon, the excellent Suvarṇabhāsa, king of sūtras." And Ratnoccaya accepted the request of King Susaṃbhava. In the whole triple-thousand world-sphere all the gods rejoiced. In a pure place, superb, excellent, with jewel-like water, sprinkled with drops of fragrant water, (**150**) he strewed the earth with flowers and then the king placed a seat there. And the king adorned[(130)] that seat with umbrellas, banners and numerous thousands of silk cloths. And the king bestrewed that seat with various excellent sandal-powders. Gods, Nāgas, Asuras, Kiṃnaras, Yakṣas, Yakṣa-kings and Mahoragas bestrewed that seat with divine showers of *māndārava*-flowers. Inconceivable thousands of millions of gods who came desirous of the Law bestrewed[(131)] Ratnoccaya as he came out with flowers from the Sāl-tree. And Ratnoccaya, the preacher of the Law, having bathed his body well, having put on pure clothing, approached that seat, (**151**) placed his hands in the gesture of reverence and did homage. The kings of

[(130)] *samalaṃkṛtaṃ* translated according to Khotanese *āysäte* (68v2 *KT* 1.241).

[(131)] *abhyākariṣyanti* is translated as preterite following K.R. Norman, *JRAS*, 1971, 198. R. Tsuchida, *CAJ*, 29, 1985, 136-137 suggests reading *abhyokireṣyanti*.

the gods, the gods and goddesses rained down *māndārava*-flowers. Inconceivable hundreds of thousands of musical instruments resounded in the sky. The monk Ratnoccaya, the preacher of the Good Law, ascended (the seat of the Law) and sat down, mindful of inconceivable thousands of millions of Buddhas in the ten directions. Producing compassion for all beings and desirous of effecting a merciful mind, he then expounded this sūtra to King Susaṃbhava. The king, having stood with his hands in the gesture of reverence, rejoiced with one accord. His eyes shed tears at the force of the Good Law. His body became full of joy. For the sake of worshipping this sūtra, King Susaṃbhava then took hold of the Cintāmaṇi, king of jewels, and made a resolve on account of the welfare of beings: "May there now rain down here in Jambudvīpa ornaments made of the seven jewels **(152)** and may the beings here in Jambudvīpa be blessed and have great riches." Then there rained down on the four continents the seven jewels, bracelets and necklaces, excellent[(132)] earrings, likewise food, drinks, and clothing. And when King Susaṃbhava saw this rain of jewels in Jambudvīpa, he presented the four continents filled with jewels to the Order of Ratnaśikhin.

And I, the Tathāgata Śākyamuni, was the king called Susaṃbhava. I then gave up the earth, the four continents full of jewels. And the Tathāgata Akṣobhya was the monk Ratnoccaya, the preacher of the Good Law, who then preached this sūtra to King Susaṃbhava. Because I heard this sūtra then and rejoiced with one accord, through that good act of mine, **(153)** and through my rejoicing at the hearing of the sūtra, I obtained a body that has the colour of gold, that has the marks of a hundred merits, always of pleasing appearance, delightful to the eyes, beautiful for people to behold, causing pleasure to thousands of millions of gods. For ninety-nine billion[(133)] aeons I was a Cakravartin-king. For numerous hundreds of thousands of aeons I experienced lesser kingship. For inconceivable aeons I was Śakra, likewise Brahma, whose mind is tranquil. Immeasurable are the Buddhas I have pleased, whose measure can never be found. So is the

[(132)] Read *varakuṇḍalāni*, Tib. *rna-cha mchog*.

[(133)] Read *navottarānavatisahasrakoṭyaḥ* (Skjærvø) i.e. 99 × 10.000.000 × 100.000.

mass of my many merits without measure, since I heard this sūtra and rejoiced in it, as according to my desire I have obtained enlightenment and have acquired the body of the Good Law. **(154)**

So (ends) the thirteenth chapter, the Chapter on Susaṃbhava, in the excellent Suvarṇabhāsa, king of sūtras.

14. Chapter on the Refuge of the Yakṣas

Great goddess Śrī, whatever faithful noble son or noble daughter should have the desire to do homage that is inconceivable, great, vast, extensive, with all appurtenances, to past, future, and present Lord Buddhas, should be desirous of knowing the profound Buddha-sphere of past, future, and present Lord Buddhas, he assuredly, in that region, monastery, or forest-region, in which this excellent Suvarṇabhāsa, king of sūtras, **(155)** is expounded in detail, must listen to this excellent Suvarṇabhāsa, king of sūtras, with concentrated mind and attentive ear.

Then indeed the Lord, illuminating this meaning in greater detail, at that time spoke these verses:

"Whoever should desire to do inconceivable honour to all the Buddhas and to know the profound sphere of all the Buddhas, he should approach that place, monastery or cell, where this excellent Suvarṇabhāsa is preached. This sūtra is an inconceivable endless ocean of virtues (and) rescues all beings from numerous oceans of woes.[(134)] **(156)** I behold the beginning of the sūtra, the middle, and the end: it is the king of sūtras, extremely profound, (and) nothing is found to compare with it. Neither the dust in the Ganges, nor on the earth, nor in the ocean, nor that found in the sky can provide comparison."

"Then he must enter, by entry into the sphere of the Law, where there is the stūpa whose nature is the Law, profound, well-established. And in the midst of this stūpa he will see the Buddha Śākyamuni expounding this sūtra in a pleasant voice. However many millions of aeons, inconceivable, incalculable periods, **(157)** he experiences

[(134)] Reading *anekair duḥkhasāgaraiḥ* with MS. H in accordance with the Tibetan versions, cf. R. Tsuchida, *CAJ*, 29, 1985, 139-140.

divine and human pleasures, one who hears this sūtra will know that an inconceivable mass of merit has been thus acquired by him. One who is capable of hearing this sūtra would traverse a hundred leagues fully covered with holes of fire. He would endure great pain. As soon as he has entered (his) monastery or cell, ills depart from him, every evil dream and sign. As soon as he has entered it, all oppressions caused by planets and asterisms, dreaded evil demons, turn away from him. He should make there such a seat resembling a lotus as the Nāga-kings revealed to him in his dream. And having sat on that seat, he will expound this sūtra. He must read what is written and likewise understand it. Getting down from the seat he will go to another place. There on that seat miracles will be seen. And at times the form of the preacher of the Law will be seen there, at times the form of the Buddha and at times a Bodhisattva. Sometimes the forms of Samantabhadra or of Mañjuśrī, sometimes forms of Maitreya are seen on that seat. Sometimes merely a glow, sometimes the appearance of gods **(158)** is glimpsed for a moment and then disappears. The Buddha's Order is everywhere, producing success, renowned, endowed with grain[(135)] and blessing. [It is a sign, an apparition of the Buddha, causing victory, fortune and fame, turning back opponents, completely defeating hordes of foreign enemies, overthrowing enemies in battle, removing all evil dreams, destroying all evils, removing all evils,[(136)]] bringing victory in battle. He will fill the whole of this Jambudvīpa with his fame, and all his enemies will be soundly defeated. His enemies will always be suppressed and he will turn away from all evil. Having conquered the vanguard, free of enemies, he rejoices."

"King Brahma, (Śakra) the Lord of the Thirty (gods), likewise the world-protectors, Vajrapāṇi, the lord of the Yakṣas, Saṃjñāya, the chief Conqueror, Anavatapta, lord of the Nāgas, likewise Sāgara, the lords of the Kiṃnaras and the lords of the Asuras, likewise the lords of the Garuḍas–with these placed at the head, all the gods **(159)** continually honour the inconceivable stūpa of the Law. When they see venerable beings they will become joyful. All the excellent lords of

(135) Read *dhānya*- Nobel, *Tib.* p.123 n.56.

(136) Translated from Tib. (p.123) as the Sanskrit is missing.

the gods will think thus, and all those gods will speak to one another: 'Look at all those (beings) endowed with brilliance, glory, and merits! Because of a purified merit-root these men have come here, who have come here in order to hear this profound sūtra, venerable men with inconceivable devotion to the stūpa of the Law. They have compassion for the world. They are working for the welfare of beings. They are a vessel for the juice of the Good Law, for profound things. Those who enter by entry into the sphere of the Law are those who hear this sūtra, the excellent Suvarṇabhāsa. (**160**) They have worshipped hundreds of thousands of former Buddhas and because of this merit-root they hear this sūtra.'"

"All these kings of the gods, likewise Sarasvatī, Śrī, Vaiśravaṇa, likewise the four kings, together with hundreds of thousands of Yakṣas possessed of supernatural powers and great strength, (**161**) will give them protection everywhere in the four directions. Indra, Soma, Vāyu, Varuṇa, Skanda, Viṣṇu, Sarasvatī, Prajāpati, and Hutāśana, all these world-protectors of great strength and prowess, will always give them protection, unwearied by day or night. And the very powerful Yakṣa-lords, Nārāyaṇa and Maheśvara and the twenty-eight others headed by Saṃjñāya, together with hundreds of thousands of Yakṣas possessed of supernatural powers and great strength, will offer them protection in all their fears and terrors. And Vajrapāṇi, lord of the Yakṣas, with five hundred Yakṣas and all the Bodhisattvas, will give them protection. Māṇibhadra, lord of the Yakṣas, likewise Pūrṇabhadra, Kumbhīra, and Āṭavaka, likewise Piṅgala and Kapila, each Yakṣa-lord with five hundred Yakṣas, will give protection to those who have heard this sūtra. Citrasena, the Gandharva, Jinarṣabha,[(137)] king of Conquerors, Maṇikaṇṭha, Nikaṇṭha, Varṣādhipati, Mahāgrāsa, Mahākāla, likewise Suvarṇakeśa, (**162**) Pāñcika, Chagalapāda, likewise Mahābhāga, Praṇālin, Dharmapāla, Markaṭa, Vāli, Sūciroma, Sūryamitra, likewise Ratnakeśa, Mahāpraṇālin, Nakula, Kāmaśreṣṭha, Candana, Nāgayana, Haimavata, likewise Satāgiri–all these, possessed of supernatural powers, great strength and prowess, will give protection to those to whom this sūtra is dear. Anavatapta, lord of the Nāgas, likewise Sāgara, both

[(137)] Jinarṣabha is the name of a Yakṣa in the Mahāmāyūrī.

Mucilinda and Elapatra, Nanda and Upanandaka, with hundreds of thousands of Nāgas, possessed of supernatural powers and great strength, will give them protection from every fear and terror. Bali, Rāhu, Namuci, Vemacitra, Saṃvara, Prahlāda, Kharaskandha, and likewise other lords of the Asuras, with hundreds of thousands of Asuras, possessed of supernatural powers and great strength, will give them protection from fear and terror that has arisen. Hārītī, mother of the Bhūtas, with her five hundred sons, will give them protection whether they are sleeping, sitting or standing. **(163)** Caṇḍā, Caṇḍālikā, likewise the Yakṣiṇī Caṇḍikā, Kuntī, and Kūṭadantī, who deprives all beings of their strength–all these, possessed of supernatural powers, great strength and prowess, will give them protection everywhere in the four directions. Sarasvatī at the head and inconceivable gods, all the gods here with Śrī at the head likewise, and the Earth-goddess, the deities of fruit, crop, and forest, river-deities (and) those inhabiting parks, trees and shrines–all these deities, with minds greatly rejoicing, will give protection to those to whom this sūtra is dear. And they will provide beings with old age, complexion, and strength. They will continually adorn them with glory, merits, brilliance, and fortune. They will remove all oppressions caused by planets and asterisms. They will destroy every misfortune, wickedness, and bad dream. And the profound and very powerful Earth-goddess **(164)** will be satisfied with the savour of the excellent Suvarṇaprabhāsa, king of sūtras. The savour of the earth will increase six million eight hundred thousand leagues as far as the diamond[(138)] layer. It will proceed a full hundred leagues downwards.[(139)] Through the power of hearing this sūtra, it will moisten the earth upwards. And all the deities stationed in the ten directions will be satisfied with the savour of the excellent Suvarṇaprabhāsa, king of sūtras. They will become more powerful, endowed with fortune, prowess and strength. They will be blessed with happiness, satisfied with various savours. Everywhere in this Jambudvīpa the deities of fruit, crop, and forest will be joyful at the exposition of this sūtra here. Crops, grasses, various flowers, various fruits, trees, parks, and forests **(165)** they will

[(138)] Read *vajra-* for *vraja-* (misprint).

[(139)] Cf. J.W. de Jong, *IIJ*, XIV, 1972, 121.

make flower beautifully and emit various perfumes. With various flowers and with various fruits, they will make grow all the grasses and trees on the earth. Everywhere in this Jambudvīpa inconceivable Nāga-girls will be joyful in mind, and approaching lotus-pools, they will plant in all the lotus-pools various kinds of lotuses, blue and white. The sky will become pure, free of smoke and masses of clouds. The quarters, with darkness and dust removed, will shine brilliantly. **(166)** The sun, shining brightly with its thousand rays, with its mass of beams, rejoicing in its deep brilliance, will rise. The lordly sun, offspring of the gods, residing in his palace of Jambūnada gold, will be satisfied by this sūtra. The lordly sun will rise in Jambudvīpa greatly rejoicing. He will shine everywhere with his endless mass of rays. As soon as he has risen, at the sending forth of his mass of rays, he will awaken the lotuses that fill the various pools. Everywhere in this Jambudvīpa he will fully and properly ripen the various crops, fruits, and plants. He will satisfy the whole earth. **(167)** Then the moon and the sun will shine with distinction. The asterisms, likewise wind and rain, will come at the proper time. There will be plenty everywhere in the whole[(140)] of Jambudvīpa, especially in that realm where this sūtra may be."

So (ends) the fourteenth chapter, the Chapter on protection, called "The Refuge of the Yakṣas", in the excellent Suvarṇabhāsa, king of sūtras.

15. Chapter on the Prophecy concerning the Ten Thousand Divine Sons

When this had been said, the noble goddess Bodhisattvasamuccayā spoke thus to the Lord: "For what cause, dear Lord, for what reason, because of whose performing, accumulating, what pure merit-root, **(168)** have these ten thousand sons of gods headed by Jvalanāntara-tejorāja now come from the dwelling of the Thirty-three[(141)] and entered the presence of the Lord in order to hear the Law?"

[(140)] Read *sarva-* Nobel, *Tib.* p.131 n.195.

[(141)] Read *trayastriṃśadbhavanād* Nobel, Nachtrag.

"For they had heard the prophecy to enlightenment[142] for the following three good persons: that this good person Ruciraketu will in future time, when numerous hundreds of thousands of millions of incalculable aeons surpassing reckoning have elapsed, awaken to supreme and perfect enlightenment in the Suvarṇaprabhāsitā world-sphere. He will be born in the world as the Tathāgata called Suvarṇaratnākaracchatrakūṭa, the Arhat, fully enlightened one, perfected in wisdom and good conduct, one who has attained bliss, having knowledge of the world, supreme charioteer of men to be trained, teacher of men and of gods, Lord Buddha. (So it will be) until, when the Lord Suvarṇaratnākaracchatrakūṭa, the Tathāgata, Arhat, fully enlightened one, has attained complete Nirvāṇa, the Good Law has disappeared, **(169)** and his teaching has altogether wholly in every way disappeared, this son called Rūpyaketu, in succession to that Tathāgata, will be born in the world in that Virajadhvaja world-sphere as the Tathāgata called Suvarṇajambudhvajakāñcanābha, the Arhat, fully enlightened one. (So it will be) until, when the Tathāgata Suvarṇajambudhvajakāñcanābha, the Arhat, fully enlightened one, has attained complete Nirvāṇa and his teaching has altogether wholly in every way disappeared, this son called Rūpyaprabha, in succession to that Tathāgata, will in that Virajadhvaja world-sphere awaken to supreme and perfect enlightenment. He will be born in the world as the Tathāgata called *Suvarṇaśataraśmiprabhāsaketu,[143] the Arhat, fully enlightened one, perfected in wisdom and good conduct, one who has attained bliss, having knowledge of the world, supreme charioteer of men to be trained, teacher of men and of gods, Lord Buddha."

"All these were now prophesied by the Lord to supreme and perfect enlightenment. **(170)** But until then, dear Lord, those ten thousand divine sons, headed by Jvalanāntaratejorāja, had not followed extensively the Bodhisattva-career. It has not previously been heard that

[142] Read *bodhi-* for *bodhisattva-* with MS. G. and in agreement with Tib. *byaṅ-chub-tu*. Cf. *bodhivyākaraṇaṃ* p.172 l.15 (same phrase).

[143] The name is probably to be so read rather than Suvarṇaśataraśmibhāsagarbha as read by Nobel since the Tibetan rendering indicates that the same name occurred here as on p.119.

they have previously behaved according to the six perfections. It has not been heard that they have previously given up hands, feet, eyes, the supreme member (the head), beloved sons, wife, daughters. It has not been heard that they have previously given up wealth, grain, gold, gems, pearls, beryl, conches, crystal, coral, silver, gold, and jewels. It has not been heard that they have previously given up food, drink, clothing, vehicles, beds, seats, dwellings, palaces. parks, ponds, and pools. It has not been heard that they have previously given up elephants, cows, horses, mares, female and male servants, just as those numerous hundreds of thousands of millions of Bodhisattvas during numerous **(171)** hundreds of thousands of millions of previous incalculable aeons will do worship with numerous, inconceivable, various hundreds of thousands of acts of worship, with all the appurtenances, to numerous incalculable hundreds of thousands of millions of Tathāgatas; will give up all objects; will give up hands, feet, eyes, the supreme member (the head), beloved sons, wife, daughters; will give up wealth, grain, gold, gems, pearls, beryl, conches, crystal, coral, silver, and gold; will give up food, drink, clothing, beds, seats, dwellings, palaces, parks, gardens, ponds, elephants, cows, horses, mares, female and male servants; will fulfill successively the six perfections; having fulfilled successively the six perfections, will experience numerous hundreds of thousands of blessings, before they will obtain from the Lord Buddha the prophecy to the name of Tathāgata.[(144)] For what reason then, dear Lord, for what cause, through what kind of pure merit-root have these ten thousand divine sons, headed by Jvalanāntaratejorāja **(172)** approached the presence of the Lord here for the hearing of the Law? (Why) has the Lord now prophesied them to supreme and perfect enlightenment, (prophesied) that in future time, when numerous hundreds of thousands of millions of incalculable aeons have elapsed, they will awaken to supreme and perfect enlightenment in the Sālendradhvajāgravatī world-sphere, one after the other, with the same family and clan, and with the same name, (that) they will be born in the world in the ten directions as ten thousand Buddhas named Prasannavadanotpalagandhakūṭa, perfected in wisdom and good conduct, having attained bliss, having knowledge

[(144)] Run on as preferred by Nobel, *Tib.* p.134 n.97.

of the world, supreme charioteers of men to be trained, teachers of men and of gods, Lord Buddhas?"

When this had been said, the Lord spoke thus to the noble goddess Bodhisattvasamuccayā: "There is, noble goddess, this reason, there is this cause, there is this pure merit-root on account of doing and accumulating which, these ten thousand divine sons, headed by Jvalanāntaratejorāja, have now come here from the dwelling of the Thirty-three to hear the Law. Hearing this prophecy to enlightenment for those three good men, as soon as they had heard it, noble goddess, they obtained exceeding[(145)] reverence, delight, and faith towards this excellent Suvarṇabhāsa, king of sūtras. **(173)** They became so long endowed with a pure mind resembling a flawless beryl; they became endowed with profound faith of mind resembling the pure, vast, extensive sky; they acquired an unlimited heap of merit; and, noble goddess, as soon as they had heard it, the ten thousand divine sons, headed by Jvalanāntaratejorāja, so long obtained exceeding[(146)] reverence and faith towards this excellent Suvarṇabhāsa, king of sūtras, and became so long endowed with a pure mind resembling a flawless beryl, until they reached the stage of prophecy. Noble goddess, through that acquisition of the merit-root due to hearing the Law and as the result of the power of a previous resolve, those ten thousand divine sons, headed by Jvalanāntaratejorāja, have now been prophesied by me to supreme and perfect enlightenment."

"And what, noble goddess, are those former resolves?"

So (ends) the fifteenth chapter, the Chapter on the Prophecy concerning the ten thousand divine sons, in the excellent Suvarṇabhāsa, king of sūtras. **(174)**

16. Chapter on Healing Illness[(147)]

Formerly, noble goddess, in past time, when incalculable (and still)

(145) Read *sūtrendrarājasyātirekacitrī* ° Nobel, *Tib.* p.135 n.128.

(146) Read *sūtrendrarājasyātirekacitrī* ° Nobel, *Tib.* p.136 n.138.

(147) For discussion of this chapter, see J. Nobel, *Ein alter medizinischer Sanskrit-Text und seine Deutung,* Supplement to *JAOS*, no.11, 1951.

more incalculable aeons,[(148)] extensive, inconceivable, immeasurable, had elapsed, at that time, at that moment, there appeared in the world a Tathāgata called Ratnaśikhin, an Arhat, fully enlightened one, perfected in wisdom and good conduct, having attained bliss, having knowledge of the world, supreme charioteer of men to be trained, teacher of men and of gods, Lord Buddha. And indeed at that time, noble goddess, at that moment, when the Lord Ratnaśikhin, the Tathāgata, Arhat, fully enlightened one, had attained complete Nirvāṇa, when the Good Law had disappeared and there was a copy of the Good Law about, there was a king called Sureśvaraprabha. A Law-abiding king of the Law he protected his realm according to the Law, not according to lawlessness. He was like a mother and father to the beings dwelling in all his districts.

Moreover, at that time, noble goddess, at that moment, there was **(175)** in the land[(149)] of King Sureśvaraprabha a merchant called Jaṭiṃdhara, a doctor, a medical man, expert in the chief elements.[(150)] He was fully versed in the eightfold[(151)] treatise[(152)] on medicine. And indeed at that time, noble goddess, at that moment, the merchant Jaṭiṃdhara had a son called Jalavāhana, a merchant's son, handsome, fair, attractive, endowed with supreme excellence of pure complexion, expert in the various treatises, adept in all the treatises, learned in writing, reckoning and counting.

And indeed at that time, noble goddess, at that moment, there were

[(148)] Read *asaṃkhyeyaiḥ kalpair asaṃkhyeyatarair* as indicated by MS. G in accord with Tibetan and Chinese. Cf. R. Tsuchida, *CAJ*, 29, 1985, 143-144.

[(149)] Read *viṣaye* for *rāṣṭre* Nobel, *Tib.* p.137 n.13.

[(150)] The six (usually seven, but six is specified in v.8) elements (*dhātu*) are the fundamental parts of the body. The seven are: *rasa* 'fluid', *rakta* 'blood', *māṃsa* 'flesh', *medas* 'fat', *asthi* 'bone', *majjā* 'marrow' and *śukra* 'semen'. Dharmakṣema and I-tsing, however, have reinterpreted *dhātu* as meaning the same as *mahābhūta*, the elements earth, water, fire, and wind.

[(151)] The eight branches of medicine were according to Suśruta: 1. *śalya* '(use of) the scalpel'; 2. *śālākya* 'use of the probe'; 3. *kāyacikitsā* 'treatment of the body'; 4. *bhūtavidyā* 'knowledge of evil spirits'; 5. *kaumārabhṛtya* 'paediatrics'; 6. *agadatantra* 'science of antidotes'; 7. *rasāyanatantra* 'science of elixirs'; 8. *vājīkaraṇatantra* 'science of aphrodisiacs'. See C. Vogel, 'On Bu-ston's view of the eight parts of Indian medicine', in *IIJ*, VI, 3/4, 1963, 290-295.

[(152)] Read *°tantreṇa* Nobel, Nachtrag.

in the land of King Sureśvaraprabha numerous hundreds of thousands of beings afflicted with various illnesses. Oppressed by their various diseases, they experienced pain that was wretched, severe, sharp, fierce, unpleasant. And indeed at that time, noble goddess, at that moment, for the sake of those numerous hundreds of thousands of beings, beings afflicted with various illnesses, oppressed by various diseases, the merchant's son Jalavāhana produced a supremely compassionate thought: "These **(176)** numerous hundreds of thousands of beings afflicted with various illnesses, oppressed by various diseases, are[(153)] now experiencing pain that is wretched, severe, sharp, fierce, unpleasant. And this father of mine, Jaṭiṃdhara, the merchant, a doctor, a medical man, expert in the chief elements, fully versed in the eightfold treatise on medicine, is old, decrepit, aged, elderly, advanced in years, leaning on a stick, trembling as he walks. He cannot go to villages, cities, settlements, districts, realms, and palaces in order to free from their various diseases those numerous hundreds of thousands of beings afflicted with various illnesses, oppressed by various diseases. What if I were now to approach my father Jaṭiṃdhara and inquire about skill in the elements involved in diseases, so that with the skill in the elements that I have inquired about I may go to all the villages, cities, settlements, districts, realms, and palaces, and having gonc, I may free from their various diseases those numerous hundreds of thousands of beings afflicted with various illnesses, oppressed by various diseases?" **(177)**

Moreover, at that time, noble goddess, at that moment, Jalavāhana, the merchant's son, approached the place where his father the merchant was. He went up to him, did homage with his head at the feet of his father Jaṭiṃdhara, placed his hands in the gesture of reverence and stood on one side. Standing on one side, Jalavāhana, the merchant's son, asked his father, the merchant Jaṭiṃdhara, about skill in the elements in the following verses:

"How do the senses fail, the elements change? At what time do diseases arise for corporeal beings? And how does one eat, in season and

(153) Omit *sma* with ABCDE.

out of season,[154] the food that brings welfare, by which the body-fire is not harmed inside the body? How is medicine to be practised in order to cure a disease when one has arisen due to wind, bile, phlegm, or a combination (of these)? At what time is wind disturbed, at what time is bile disturbed, at what time is phlegm disturbed, so that men are oppressed?" **(178)**

Then indeed the merchant Jaṭiṃdhara expounded skill in the elements to the merchant's son Jalavāhana in these verses:

"The rainy season is seen to be three months, autumn is said to be three, winter likewise three, and three too the hot season. Thus the succession of months (forms) six periods. A year is said to have twelve months. ...[155] The monthly period is to be viewed in twos. Food and drink are consumed accordingly. And the doctor, his skill, and the period, have been explained. And the senses and elements change during the divisions of the year. **(179)** The senses changing, the various diseases arise for corporeal beings. In that case, the doctor must have skill concerning the fourfold division into three months, the six periods in the (bimonthly) division, and the six elements. Food, drink, and medicine are according to this sequence. Illnesses due to excess of wind occur in the rainy season. Disturbance of the bile is taught[156] (to occur) in autumn. Likewise, (illness) due to a combination (arises) in winter-time. Illnesses due to excess of phlegm arise in the hot season. In the rainy season, the (characteristic) tastes (are) fatty, warm, salty, and sour; in autumn seasons, fatty, sweet, and cold; in winter-time, sweet, sour, and fatty; and in summer-time, rough, warm, and bitter. **(180)** Excess of phlegm erupts as soon as one has eaten. Excess of bile erupts during digestion. Excess of wind erupts as soon as one has digested. In this manner do the three elements erupt. Give strengthening to one who has wind, a purgative

[154] Reading *kālākāle* (cf. MS. G) as implied by the Tibetan version (Nobel, *Tib.* p.139 n.64).

[155] The Sanskrit text is here defective. The Tibetan version has *gsum-gsum-du ni ćhigs-rnams bsdus-par śes* 'The divisions (of the year) [i.e. Sanskrit *parvan*] are known to be grouped in threes.' The fragmentary Khotanese has *drai drai biśvo rvo'* 'by threes in all the seasons'.

[156] Reading *praśasyate* following MS. G (*prasasyate*). Most MSS. have *prasanne*, which does not yield acceptable sense: 'in the clear autumn' (?).

to remove[157] bile, in the case of a combination (give) something endowed with the three qualities, and one should use an emetic during a period of (excess) phlegm. One must know in which periods excess of wind, bile or a combination, (or) excess of phlegm (occur). That food, drink, or medicine must be prescribed which accords with the time, the element, and the person."

Then indeed Jalavāhana, the merchant's son, having inquired about [158] skill in the elements connected with the underlying causes (of illnesses), understood the whole eightfold medical knowledge. **(181)**

And indeed at that time, noble goddess, at that moment, Jalavāhana, the merchant's son, went to all the villages, cities, settlements, districts, realms, and palaces in the land of King Sureśvaraprabha and thus comforted all those numerous hundreds of thousands of beings afflicted with various illnesses, oppressed by various diseases: "I am a doctor, I am a doctor." So did he advertise himself. "I will free you from your various diseases."

As soon as they heard, noble goddess, Jalavāhana, the merchant's son, uttering such words as these, all those numerous hundreds of thousands of millions of beings became full of great joy. They became comforted, endowed with inconceivable joy and gladness. At that time, at that moment, through their rejoicing, numerous hundreds of thousands of millions of beings afflicted with various illnesses, oppressed by various diseases, were freed from their various illnesses. And they became without illness and free from disease.[159] They became endowed with such energy, strength, and prowess as before.[160]

And indeed at that time, noble goddess, at that moment, among

[157] Reading *°nivartanārtham* as Nobel, Sanskrit text, p.180 n.15.

[158] As pointed out by J.W. de Jong (*IIJ*, XIV, 1972, 121), the Tibetan *de ćam-źig* indicates a Sanskrit reading *tanmātrakeṇa* (cf. MS. G *mattikena*). However, the better attested MS. reading *naimittikena* should be retained. The medical lore that has been presented falls in fact into the category of *nidāna* or *nimitta* 'underlying cause'.

[159] Read *vigata-vyādhīni ca* with MS. J (Skjærvø). *vigata-vyādhīni* is indicated also by the MSS. ABCDEF and is supported by Khotanese *jya-āchā*.

[160] Reading *yathā-paurāṇena sthāma-bala-vīryeṇa samanvāgatāni babhūvuḥ* as indicated by the MSS. and confirmed by the fragmentary Khotanese version. Nobel relegated the sentence to the apparatus (p.181 n.41).

those hundreds of thousands of millions of beings afflicted with various illnesses, oppressed by various diseases, whoever were afflicted with a severe illness all came to Jalavāhana, the merchant's son. And having come, whatever (**182**) medical prescriptions Jalavāhana, the merchant's son, enjoined upon those numerous hundreds of thousands of millions of beings afflicted with various illnesses, oppressed by various diseases, all the diseases of all those beings were thus removed. And they became without illness or with slight disease, and endowed with such energy, strength and prowess as before.

And indeed at that time, noble goddess, at that moment, in all the villages, cities, settlements, districts, realms, and palaces in the land of King Sureśvaraprabha, all those numerous hundreds of thousands of millions of beings afflicted with various illnesses, oppressed by various diseases, were freed from their various diseases by the merchant's son Jalavāhana.

So (ends) the sixteenth chapter, the Chapter on Healing Illness, in the excellent Suvarṇabhāsa, king of sūtras.

17. Chapter on Jalavāhana

Moreover, noble goddess, all the beings in the land of King Sureśvaraprabha were made without illness or with slight disease by the merchant's son Jalavāhana and became as before in energy, strength, and body. (**183**) In the land of King Sureśvaraprabha all the beings rejoiced, played, enjoyed themselves, gave gifts, and performed merits. They honoured the merchant's son Jalavāhana: "May he be victorious, may the merchant's son Jalavāhana be victorious, the great king of doctors, the healer of the diseases of all beings. He must surely be a visible Bodhisattva. He has understood the whole eightfold medical knowledge."

And indeed, noble goddess, Jalavāhana, the merchant's son, had a wife named Jalāmbugarbhā. And indeed, noble goddess, Jalāmbugarbhā had two sons. One was called Jalāmbara, the other Jalagarbha. (**184**)

Then indeed, noble goddess, Jalavāhana, the merchant's son, together with his two sons, visited successively the villages, cities, settlements, districts, realms, and palaces. Then indeed, noble goddess, at a later time Jalavāhana, the merchant's son, arrived at a certain forest wilderness. Then he saw in that forest wilderness flesh-eating dogs, wolves, jackals, and flocks of crows and (other) birds.[(161)] They ran in that direction where there was the pool Aṭavīsaṃbhavā ("arising in the forest"). It thus occurred to him: "For what reason are these flesh-eating dogs, wolves, jackals, and flocks of crows and (other) birds running in this direction?" It thus occurred to him: "What if I were now to approach that region in which (**185**) direction the flesh-eating dogs, wolves, jackals, and flocks of crows and (other) birds[(162)] are running?" Then indeed, noble goddess, Jalavāhana, the merchant's son, going about in the course of his successive visiting, reached that place where there was the pool Aṭavīsaṃbhavā.

In that great pool there live ten thousand fish. There he saw many hundreds of fish deprived of water. There he produced a compassionate thought. He saw there a goddess coming out of a tree with half her body only. That goddess spoke thus to the merchant's son Jalavāhana: "Bravo, bravo, noble son. Since you are called Jalavāhana ("water bringer"), give water to the fish. For two reasons is one called Jalavāhana: because one brings water and because one gives water. Therefore act according to your name." Jalavāhana said: "How many, goddess, are those fish?" The goddess said: "There are full ten thousand fish." Then indeed, noble goddess, Jalavāhana, the merchant's son, produced in great measure supremely compassionate thought.

And at that moment, noble goddess, in the pool Aṭavīsaṃbhavā (**186**) there was only a little water left. Then those ten thousand fish, having come to death's door, deprived of water, darted about. Then indeed, noble goddess, Jalavāhana, the merchant's son, ran in the four directions. In whatever direction Jalavāhana, the merchant's son, went, in that direction the ten thousand fish looked pitiably upon Jalavāhana. Then indeed, noble goddess, Jalavāhana, the merchant's son, ran in the four directions in search of water, but he did not find

[(161)] Reading °*kāka-pakṣi-gaṇā* as below cf. the following footnote. The fragmentary Khotanese has *[mu]rāṇu ttāmäre* 'flocks (?) of birds'.

[(162)] Reading °*kāka-pakṣi-gaṇā* cf. Nobel p.184 n.19. The Khotanese has *[ṣ]ṣundä mura gge'jsa* 'crows, birds in a flock'.

water there. He looked in the four directions. He saw not far off a great mass of trees. Climbing those trees and cutting off branches, he approached the pool. Having approached, with those tree branches he made very cool[(163)] shade for those ten thousand fish.

Then indeed, noble goddess, Jalavāhana, the merchant's son, investigated the arrival of water into the pool, whence the water might come. He ran in the four directions, and he did not find water. Very quickly he followed the stream. And indeed, noble goddess, from that pool Aṭavīsaṃbhavā (**187**) there was a great river called Jalāgamā, whence the water came into it. And at that moment this river had been made to fall into a great hole in such a place by a certain evil being on account of those ten thousand fish so that there would be no further arrival of water for those fish. Seeing this, he thought: "Not even a thousand men could bring the river by this path, how much less then could I alone bring it?" He went back.

Then indeed, noble goddess, Jalavāhana, the merchant's son, proceeding very quickly, approached King Sureśvaraprabha. Having approached he did homage with his head at the feet of King Sureśvaraprabha and sat down on one side. He informed him of this news: "I have indeed allayed[(164)] the illnesses of the beings in all villages, cities, (**188**) settlements, realms, and palaces in Your Majesty's land. In a certain place there is a pool called Aṭavīsaṃbhavā. There dwell ten thousand fish, deprived of water, scorched by the sun. May Your Majesty give me twenty elephants so that I may give to those who are in the animal state life such as is given to men." Then King Sureśvaraprabha ordered his ministers: "Give to the great king of doctors twenty elephants." The ministers said: "Go to the elephant-house, great being. Take twenty elephants. Act for the welfare of beings."

Then indeed, noble goddess, the merchant's son Jalavāhana, together with his sons Jalāmbara and Jalagarbha, took twenty elephants from the elephant-keepers. Taking a hundred leather bags, he returned to where (**189**) the great river called Jalāgamā flows.

[(163)] Read *suśītalāṃ* for Nobel's *suśītalaṃ* (misprint).

[(164)] Read *prasrambhitāḥ* as implied by the MSS. for Nobel's *praśamitāḥ* (R. Tsuchida, *CAJ*, 29, 1985, 144.

Having come there, he filled those leather bags with water, raised the water on the back of the elephants and went very quickly to the pool Aṭavīsaṃbhavā. Having come, he took the water down from the back of the elephants, filled the pool in the four directions with water and walked about in the four directions. Wherever Jalavāhana, the merchant's son, went, those ten thousand fish hastened after him.

Then indeed, noble goddess, this thought occurred to Jalavāhana, the merchant's son: "Why do these ten thousand fish hasten after me?" Next this occurred to him: "No doubt these fish, oppressed by the fire of hunger, are seeking food from me. What if I were now to give them food?"

Then indeed, noble goddess, Jalavāhana, the merchant's son, spoke thus to his son Jalāmbara: "Go, noble son, to your own dwelling, mounting the swiftest elephant of all, **(190)** and having arrived very quickly, speak thus to your grandfather the merchant: 'Grandfather, Jalavāhana speaks thus: "Whatever food may be ready in this house for parents, brothers, sisters, female and male servants, and workmen, make it all into a single bundle, put it on Jalāmbara's elephant and despatch him quickly to Jalavāhana."'"

Then indeed his son Jalāmbara mounted the elephant and went off very quickly. He approached his own dwelling, and having approached it, he made known this message to his grandfather in detail. The grandfather despatched everything as previously mentioned to Jalāmbara. Then indeed his son Jalāmbara raised this food upon the elephant's back, **(191)** mounted the elephant and went to the pool Aṭavīsaṃbhavā. Jalavāhana saw that his son Jalāmbara had arrived,[(165)] and seeing him, he was contented and happy. He took the food from his son, chopped it up, threw it in that pool and satisfied those ten thousand fish. Thus it occurred to him: **(192)** "It has been heard by me that at another moment of time in a forest retreat a monk maintaining the Mahāyāna said: 'Whoever should at the time of death hear the name of the Tathāgata Ratnaśikhin, the Arhat, the fully enlightened one,[(166)] will be reborn in the blissful world of heaven.' What if I were now to expound to those fish the profound Law of origina-

[(165)] Reading *āgataṃ* with the MSS.

[(166)] Reading *arhataḥ samyaksaṃbuddhasya* in accordance with the MSS.

tion by dependence? I will make them hear the name of the Tathāgata Ratnaśikhin, the Arhat, the fully enlightened one."

And at that moment in Jambudvīpa the views of beings were twofold: some believed in the Mahāyāna, others despised it. Then indeed (**193**) at that time Jalavāhana, the merchant's son, placed both his feet in that pool as far as the knee and solemnly spoke thus: "Homage to the Lord Ratnaśikhin, the Tathāgata, the Arhat, the fully enlightened one, who, while formerly practising the Bodhisattva-career, made this resolve: 'Whoever in the ten directions should at the time of death hear my name will transmigrate thence and will be reborn to the same lot as the Thirty-three gods.'"

Then indeed Jalavāhana, the merchant's son, expounded this Law[(167)] to those who were in the animal state: "When this arises from this, from the origination of this, this originates. Now, predispositions are the result of ignorance. Consciousness is the result of predisposition. Individuality is the result of consciousness. The six senses are the result of individuality. Contact is the result of the six senses. Feeling is the result of contact. Craving is the result of feeling. Grasping is the result of craving. Arising is the result of grasping. Birth is the result of arising. As the result of birth there arise old age, death, grief, lamentation, woe, despair, and trouble. Thus is the origin of this whole great mass of evil. Now, from the cessation of ignorance comes the cessation of predispositions; from the cessation of predispositions, (**194**) the cessation of consciousness; from the cessation of consciousness, the cessation of individuality; from the cessation of individuality, the cessation of the six senses; from the cessation of the six senses, the cessation of contact; from the cessation of contact, the cessation of feeling; from the cessation of feeling, the cessation of

[(167)] There follows a detailed statement of the doctrine generally known as 'the chain of causation', alluded to above (**61**). For this the technical name is *pratītya-samutpāda* 'origination by dependence', which occurs at (195[6]) and (200[16]). On this doctrine see F. Th. Stcherbatsky, *Buddhist Logic*, vol. I, New York 1962 (reprint), pp.134 ff.; F. Bernhard, 'Zur Interpretation der Pratītyasamutpāda-Formel', *WZKSO*, XII-XIII, 1968/69, 53-63 (Festschrift für Erich Frauwallner); Geshe Lhundub Sopa, 'The Tibetan "Wheel of Life": iconography and doxography', *JIABS*, 7.1, 1984, 125-145; id. 'The special theory of the cycle of dependent origination', *JIABS*, 9.1, 1986, 105-119.

craving; from the cessation of craving, the cessation of grasping; from the cessation of grasping, the cessation of arising; from the cessation of arising, the cessation of birth; from the cessation of birth, the cessation of old age, death, grief, lamentation, woe, despair, and trouble. Thus is the cessation of this whole great mass of evil." So, noble goddess, did Jalavāhana, the merchant's son, at that time, at that moment, preach this sermon on the Law to those who were in the animal state. And then he returned to his home with his sons Jalāmbara and Jalagarbha.

Then at a later period of time Jalavāhana, the merchant's son, having enjoyed a great festival, lay on his bed intoxicated with intoxicating liquor. At that time, at that moment, the appearance of a great sign occurred, when, at the end of the night those ten thousand fish, having died, were reborn to the same lot among the Thirty-three gods. **(195)** And as soon as they had been reborn, there arose in their mind a reflection of the following kind: "By reason of what good act have we been reborn here among the Thirty-three gods?" It occurred thus to them: "In that Jambudvīpa we were ten thousand fish. While we were in the animal state we were satisfied with abundant water by the merchant's son Jalavāhana and with excellent food. And he preached to us the profound Law of origination by dependence and made us hear the name of the Tathāgata Ratnaśikhin, the Arhat, the fully enlightened one. By reason of that good act, for that reason, we have been reborn here among the gods. Wherefore now we will go to Jalavāhana, the merchant's son. Having gone, we will do homage to him." Then those ten thousand divine sons disappeared from among the Thirty-three gods. They stood in the house of the merchant's son Jalavāhana.

And indeed at that moment, Jalavāhana, the merchant's son, was lying on his bed. Those divine sons placed ten thousand pearl necklaces beside his head. They placed ten thousand pearl necklaces at the sole of his foot. They placed ten thousand pearl necklaces at his right side. They placed ten thousand pearl necklaces at his left side. **(196)** There rained down a great shower of *mandāra*-flowers and *mahāmandāra*-flowers. And divine drums were struck so that all the men in Jambudvīpa awoke. And Jalavāhana, the merchant's son, awoke. Then the ten thousand divine sons came along the path of birds, and the divine sons, raining down a rain of *māndārava*-flowers in different places in the land of King Sureśvaraprabha, came to the pool Aṭavīsaṃbhavā. Raining down on that great pool a great shower of *māndārava*-flowers, they disappeared in that very spot. Having returned to their abode among the gods, they rejoiced there with the five qualities of desire, played and frolicked. They experienced great glory and good fortune. And in Jambudvīpa night turned to day.

Then indeed King Sureśvaraprabha inquired of his astrologers and high officials: "Why (**197**) did those signs appear last night?" They said: "May it please Your Majesty to know: in the house of the merchant's son Jalavāhana there rained down forty thousand pearl necklaces and there descended divine showers of *māndārava*-flowers." The king said: "Sirs, summon Jalavāhana, the merchant's son, with kind words." Then the astrologers and high officials went to Jalavāhana's house, and having gone, spoke thus to Jalavāhana, the merchant's son: "King Sureśvaraprabha has invited you."

Then Jalavāhana, the merchant's son, together with the high officials, went to King Sureśvaraprabha. The king asked: "Jalavāhana, do you know why such signs[(168)] appeared last night?" Then Jalavāhana, the merchant's son, spoke thus to King Sureśvaraprabha: "I know, (**198**) Your Majesty. Assuredly it was the ten thousand fish who have died." The king said: "How do you know?" Jalavāhana said: "Let Jalāmbara go, Your Majesty, to the pool and see whether those ten thousand fish are alive or dead." The king said: "So be it." Then Jalavāhana, the merchant's son, spoke thus to his son Jalāmbara: "Go, son, look in the pool Aṭavīsaṃbhavā (and see) whether those ten thousand fish are alive or dead."

Then Jalāmbara his son went very quickly to the pool Aṭavīsaṃbhavā, and approaching it, he saw that those ten thousand fish had died. And seeing a great shower of *māndārava*-flowers, he returned again and said to his father: "They are dead."

Then Jalavāhana, the merchant's son, hearing these words from his son Jalāmbara, went to King Sureśvaraprabha and revealed this news in detail: "May it please Your Majesty to know that the ten thousand fish are dead and have been reborn among the Thirty-three gods. It

[(168)] Deleting *śubha*- as Nobel, Nachtrag.

was by their (**199**) power[(169)] over us that such auspicious signs appeared last night, that in our house forty thousand pearl necklaces and divine *māndārava*-flowers were rained down." Then the king became joyful, contented, delighted, happy.

Then indeed the Lord again spoke thus to the noble goddess Bodhisattvasamuccayā: "If, noble goddess, you should think then that he was another, he was at that time, at that moment, the king called Sureśvaraprabha. Yet again it is not to be viewed thus. Why is that? Daṇḍapāṇi the Śākyan was at that time, at that moment, the king called Sureśvaraprabha. If, noble goddess, you should think then that he was another, he was at that time, at that moment, the merchant called Jaṭiṃdhara. (**200**) Yet again it is not to be viewed thus. Why is that? King Śuddhodana was at that time, at that moment, the merchant called Jaṭiṃdhara. If, noble goddess, you should think then that he was another, he was at that time, at that moment, the merchant's son called Jalavāhana. Yet again it is not to be viewed thus. Why is that? *I* was at that time, at that moment, Jalavāhana, the merchant's son. If, noble goddess, you should think then that she was another, she was at that time, at that moment, his wife called Jalāmbugarbhā. Yet again it is not to be viewed thus. Why is that? Gopā, the Śākya daughter, was at that time, at that moment, the wife of Jalavāhana, the merchant's son, called Jalāmbugarbhā. Rāhula was at that time, at that moment, his son called Jalāmbara. The noble Ānanda was at that time, at that moment, his son called Jalagarbha. If, noble goddess, you should think then that they were others, they were at that time, at that moment, the ten thousand fish. Yet again it is not to be viewed thus. Why is that? Those ten thousand divine sons, headed by Jvalanāntaratejorāja, were at that time, at that moment, the ten thousand fish, who were satisfied with water and with excellent food by me and to whom I preached the profound Law of origination by dependence, and whom I made to hear the name of the Tathāgata Ratnaśikhin, the Arhat, the fully enlightened one. By reason of that good act they have come here to me, where I have now prophesied them to supreme and perfect enlightenment. Because of their great (**201**) reverence in

[(169)] Read *anubhāvena* for *anubhavena* Nobel, Nachtrag (misprint).

hearing the Law with delight, faith, and joy, they have all[170] obtained prophecies and names. If, noble goddess, you should think then that she was another, she was at that time, at that moment, the tree-goddess. It is not to be viewed thus. Why is that? *You*, noble goddess, were at that time, at that moment, the tree-goddess."

"By this means, noble goddess, must it thus be made known that while I was revolving in the cycle of existence, I ripened many beings to enlightenment, who will all attain the stage of prophecy to supreme and perfect enlightenment."

So (ends) the seventeenth chapter, the chapter on the previous life of Jalavāhana's fish-disciples, in the excellent Suvarṇabhāsa, king of sūtras.

18. Chapter on the Tigress

Afterwards, noble goddess, as a Bodhisattva I had to sacrifice myself for the sake of the welfare of others. How was that? **(202)**

Spreading out over heaven and earth rays of hundreds of pure, vast, various virtues, with unobstructed knowledge and perception, power and prowess, the Lord, attended by a thousand monks, wandering in his course through the districts in the districts of the Pāñcālas, arrived at a certain[171] part of a wood. There he saw a region of the earth adorned with various flowers on a green, soft, dark, grassy surface.[172] And having seen it, the Lord called to the venerable Ānanda: "This region of the earth is beautiful, Ānanda, and in it is **(203)** the mark of blessing for a sermon. Make ready now the Tathāgata's seat." Then he made the seat ready according to the Lord's command. And having made it ready, he spoke thus to the Lord:

"The seat is ready. Be seated, Lord, supreme one, excellent, giver of boons to men, matchless, bringer of deliverance. May sermons on the supreme nectar be sent forth for the welfare of men, o you who have been released from the bondage of existence."

Then the Lord sat down on that seat and summoned the monks:

(170) Reading *sarvaiḥ* following MS. G.

(171) Reading *anyatara-* (cf. MS. G) with Nobel, *Tib.* p.154 n.12.

(172) Read *-tala-* (for *-tata-*) Nobel, Nachtrag.

"Do you desire then, monks, to see the relics of the Bodhisattva, who has performed difficult acts?"

When this had been said, the monks spoke thus to the Lord: "This time, best of seers, has come, chief of excellent beings, for us to see the relics of him who delighted in calm and restraint, who excelled in patience and fortitude, who delighted in a mind of recollection, who was established in unlimited virtues. Tell[(173)] this well." **(204)**

Then the Lord struck the surface of the earth with his hand, whose palm was marked with a thousand-spoked wheel[(174)] and which was as soft[(175)] as a blossoming[(176)] new lotus. And as soon as it had been struck, the earth moved in six ways. And there arose thence a stūpa made of jewels, gold, and silver. Then the Lord summoned the venerable Ānanda: "Open this stūpa, Ānanda." Then the venerable Ānanda, hearing the Lord, opened the stūpa. There he saw a container made of gold, covered with gold ornaments, gems, and pearls. And seeing it, he spoke thus to the Lord: "Lord, a container made of gold has risen up." The Lord **(205)** said: "These are seven containers. Let them all be opened." And he accordingly opened them all. There he saw relics whose colour resembled snow or white water-lilies. And seeing them, he spoke thus to the Lord: "Lord, there are relics present." The Lord said: "Bring hither, Ānanda, the relics of the great being." Then, taking those relics, the venerable Ānanda brought them to the Lord Buddha. And the Lord took hold of the relics, put them down before the assembly and said:

"These were the bones of one endowed with a mass of excellent virtues, with rare restraint, meditation, and patience, good mind, energy and fame, who has continually acted more and more with his mind on full enlightenment, of one whose energy was steadfast, of one who was resolute, and of one who delighted always in liberality." **(206)**

Then the Lord summoned the monks: "Worship, monks, the Bodhisattva's relics, which are fragrant with morality and virtue, which are

(173) Sanskrit *ghaṭṭa* is perhaps 'touch upon'. In Tib. I *śod* 'tell' must be read.

(174) The second major mark (*lakṣaṇa*). See also **(99)**.

(175) The fifth major mark (*lakṣaṇa*).

(176) Read *sphuṭita-* Nobel, *Tib.* p.155 n.49.

extremely difficult[177] to behold, and which have become fields of merit."[178] Then the monks put their hands in the gesture of reverence and with converted minds did homage with their head to those relics.

Then the venerable Ānanda, placing his hands in the gesture of reverence, spoke thus to the Lord: "The Lord, the Tathāgata, has risen above the whole world (and therefore) is worshipped by all beings. But how is it the Tathāgata worships these bones?" Then the Lord spoke thus to the venerable Ānanda: "It is because of these bones, Ānanda, that I quickly thus awoke to supreme and perfect enlightenment."

"Formerly, Ānanda, in past time, there was a king called Mahāratha, who was possessed of much wealth, grain, chariots, power, and whose power and prowess were unobstructed. He had three sons who resembled princes of the gods: Mahāpraṇāda, Mahādeva, and Mahāsattva. **(207)**

"Then the king went out to a place in a park for sport. And the princes, through their attachment to the virtues of this park and through their desire for flowers, running to and fro, entered the great Dvādaśavanagulma forest. Then when the king's sons had gone off, the princes' servants went off by themselves, dismissed by the princes. They entered the Dvādaśavanagulma in the great, protected park. Then Mahāpraṇāda spoke to his two brothers: 'Fear enters my heart. Come, let us not find destruction here by wild beasts.' Mahādeva said: 'I have no fear, except of separation from my beloved folk. This thought prevails in my heart.' Mahāsattva said: **(208)**

"'I have no fear here nor even anxiety in this opening in the forest, praised by seers, lonely. This heart of mine rejoices on account of the acquisition of supreme, vast, great benefits.'

"Then the princes, wandering about in that opening in the Dvādaśavanagulma, saw such a tigress as had given birth seven days ago, surrounded by her five offspring, tortured by hunger and thirst, her body extremely weak. And seeing her, Mahāpraṇāda said: 'Ah, alas, this wretch will have given birth six or seven days ago. **(209)** If she

[177] i.e. because they are unparalleled.

[178] On the term *puṇyakṣetra,* see É. Lamotte, *La concentration de la marche héroïque (Śūraṃgamasamādhisūtra)*, Brussels 1965, pp.231-233.

does not now find food, she will devour her own cubs or will die of starvation.' Mahāsattva said: 'What food (would suit) this wretch?' Mahāpraṇāda said: 'Warm flesh and hot blood would be what is said here to be the food of [179]tigers, hyenas, bears, and lions.' Mahādeva said: 'This wretch here has a body afflicted with hunger and thirst, has little life left, and is very weak. She cannot search for food in her position. Who would sacrifice himself for the sake of saving her life?' Mahāpraṇāda said: 'Difficult, good fellow, is self-sacrifice.' Mahāsattva said: 'This course is difficult for small-minded people like us who are attached to life and body, but for others embarked upon self-sacrifice, good people devoted to the welfare of others, it is not difficult. Moreover:' **(210)**

"'Noble beings, rising out of pity and compassion,[180] take up their body in heaven and here on earth. A hundred times without changing here, they work with joyful minds for the sake of the life of others.'

"Then the princes, extremely depressed, examined the tigress for a long time without blinking and set off. Then this occurred to Mahāsattva: 'It is now time for my self-sacrifice. Why?'

"'For a very long time has this putrid body been maintained with very costly beds, clothes, drink, food, and vehicles. Characterized by decay and ruin, finally splitting itself up, having an evil end, it does not for the first time give up its own nature, ungrateful (as it is).'

"'Moreover: **(211)** There is nothing to be gained from it because it is wholly impure.[181] I will now use it in a good act. Therefore it will be for me a boat for crossing the ocean of birth and death. Moreover:'

"'Sacrificing (this) body, which has become an abscess, possessed of hundreds of existences, loaded with excrement and urine, without substance, like foam, bearing hundreds of worms, consuming its acts, I will obtain the body of the Law, which is free of grief, changeless, without agglomerations, pure, fully endowed with virtues such as

(179) Read *vyāghratarkṣuṛkṣasiṃhānāṃ* as indicated by MSS. ABCDEF and confirmed by the Tibetan version. Nobel's addition of *eṇa* 'antelope' and *gṛdhra* 'vulture' is based on MS. G alone. F. Weller (*OLZ*, 69.7/8, 393) pointed out that *eṇa* are not carnivorous.

(180) Read *-karuṇā-* for *-karuṇa-* Nobel, *Tib.* p.158 n.147 (misprint).

(181) Read with R. Tsuchida, *CAJ*, 29, 1985, 145 *sarvato 'medhyabhūtatvāt* as implied by the MSS.

meditation, loaded with hundreds of virtues, flawless.' (**212**)

"Having thus made up his mind, his heart full of excellent compassion, he distracted those two: 'You two go off. I will enter the Dvādaśavanagulma on my own business.'

"Then Prince Mahāsattva returned from that part of the forest, went to the abode of the tigress, laid aside his clothing on a forest creeper and made a resolve:

"'For the sake of the welfare of the world, desirous of awakening to matchless, blessed enlightenment, out of compassion, with unwavering mind, I give up my body, which it is so hard for others to sacrifice. (**213**) May I obtain enlightenment, which is free of disease, revered by the Buddha-sons, free of illness. May I deliver the triple world from the ocean of existence, from fear.'

"Then Mahāsattva fell down before the tigress. Then the tigress did nothing to the compassionate Bodhisattva. Then the Bodhisattva, thinking: 'She is weak, alas, and incapable,' rose up and looked for a knife. The merciful-minded one nowhere found a knife. Taking hold of a very strong bamboo-stick, a hundred years old, and with it cutting open his throat, he fell down before the tigress. And as soon as the Bodhisattva had fallen down, (**214**) this earth, like a ship buffeted by the wind in the midst of the ocean, shook in six ways. The sun, as if devoured by Rāhu, did not shine with its rays. And a rain of flowers, mingled with divine perfumes and powders, fell down.

"Then a certain goddess, her mind overcome with amazement, praised the Bodhisattva:

"'As your compassion, good-minded one, has gone forth here to all beings, as you sacrifice joyfully your body here, hero among men, here you will, free from trouble, peaceful, attain ere long the blessed, excellent, fair place that is devoid of the meaning of birth and death.'

"Then indeed the tigress, seeing the Bodhisattva, whose body was smeared with blood, in a mere flash left only the bones, without flesh or blood. (**215**)

"Then Mahāpraṇāda, perceiving the earthquake, spoke thus to Mahādeva:

"'As this earth with its seas as far as the ocean shook in the ten directions and the sun has been robbed of its rays, a shower of flowers has fallen, and my mind is troubled, my brother has now given up[(182)] his body here.'

"Mahādeva said: 'And as he spoke with compassionate voice when he saw (the tigress) ready to devour her own cubs, full of hunger, consumed[(183)] by hundreds of troubles, my mind is very weak (and) I have doubt here.'[(184)] **(216)**

"Then the two princes, overcome with extreme grief, their eyes suffused with tears, went back along that very path and came to the very presence of the tigress. They saw all his clothing laid upon a bamboo shoot, his bones filthy with blood, scattered about, and his hair dispersed in the various directions and subdirections. Seeing this, they became faint and fell down to the ground upon his bones. When, regaining consciousness after a very long time, they stood up, with arms upraised they uttered a wretched cry:

"'Alas for our beloved brother and the king, likewise for his mother, who was devoted to her son. His mother will ask us: "Where is the third one of you, he whose eyes are long like the lotus?" **(217)**

"'Alas, better for us in this part of the earth would be death than life. How will we, without Mahāsattva, look at our mother and father?'

"Then the two princes set off, lamenting pitiably in many various ways.[(185)] Then the servants of the prince, running about in the directions and subdirections in search of the prince, on seeing each other, asked: 'Where is the prince? Where is the prince?'

"And at that moment the queen, lying on top of her bed, saw a dream showing separation from a loved one. It was like this. Her breasts were being cut off and her teeth were being wrenched out. The three young doves she was holding were afraid and one was being seized by a falcon. **(218)** Then when her heart was terrified by the earthquake, the queen suddenly woke up and became lost in thought:

[(182)] Read *visṛṣṭaḥ* for Nobel's *vissṛṭaḥ* (misprint).

[(183)] The MSS. imply a reading *saṃtāpitāṃ* R. Tsuchida, *CAJ*, 29, 1985, 145.

[(184)] Reading *sudurbalā matir iva saṃśayo 'tra me* as suggested by F. Edgerton, *Buddhist Hybrid Sanskrit Grammar and Dictionary*, vol.2: *Dictionary,* New Haven 1953, s.v. *saṃśayālu.*

[(185)] Read *bahuvividhaṃ* Nobel, Nachtrag.

"'Why does this sustainer of beings, whose garments are the oceans, shake violently? The sun has been robbed of its rays, pointing as it were to the sorrow[186] in my breast. (**219**) My limbs cause me distress. My eye quivers, and my breast is as it were cut off. May there be for me the well-being of my sons, who went for sport into that forest clearing.'

"And then when she was so reflecting, a servant, whose heart was agitated, entered and informed the queen: 'Queen, the attendants of the prince are searching for the prince. It is heard that your beloved son has perished.' And as soon as she had heard this, the queen, her heart trembling, her eyes and face full of tears, went up to the king and said: 'Lord, it is heard that my beloved son has perished.' The king too, his heart trembling, was reduced to supreme distress: 'Alas, woe! I have been separated from my beloved son.'

"Then the king comforted the queen: 'Do not be distressed, good queen. We will be energetic in searching for the prince.' Many people there having set out in search of the prince (and) having given up,[187] (**220**) then after a short time the king saw the two princes coming from afar. Having seen them, the king said: 'The princes appear, but not all of them. Alas, woe! Certainly I am bereaved of my son.'

"'Joy does not so arise for men on gaining a son as misery arises from loss of a son. Surely indeed blessed are they who are childless[188] in this world or those men who have reached death with their sons still living.'

"Then the queen, overcome with extreme grief, like a she-camel smitten in her vital part, uttered a wretched cry:

"'If my three sons with their band of servants have entered the forest clearing full of flowers, where is the third, who is like my own heart, my fine son, if my youngest does not come?' (**221**)

"And when those two had arrived, the king, who was eager to question them, questioned the two princes: 'Where is (our) youngest son?' Then, afflicted with grief, their eyes clouded by tears, their

(186) Reading *°śucaṃ* for *°bhūjaṃ* as suggested by Nobel, Sanskrit text, p.218 n.11, corresponding to Tib. *mya-ṅan*.

(187) Reading *'vibhūte* with R. Tsuchida, *CAJ*, 29, 1985, 146.

(188) Reading *'naputrāḥ* as suggested by R. Tsuchida, *CAJ*, 29, 1985, 147.

palates, lips, teeth, and mouths parched, those two said nothing. The queen said:

"'Speak at once. My mind fails me, and my body is very severely oppressed. Where is the third one, my beloved son? This heart of mine desires as it were to burst.'

"Then the two princes made known the occurrence in detail. As soon as they had heard it, the king and the queen became senseless. And as soon as they had returned to their senses, weeping in a pitiful voice, they went to that place. Then the king and the queen, seeing his bones without blood, flesh or sinews, and his hairs scattered in the directions and subdirections, fell to the ground like trees buffeted by the wind. Then the priest and the ministers, **(222)** seeing the situation, revived the body of the king and of the queen with water and salves of Malaya-sandal. Then, regaining consciousness after a very long while, the king rose up and lamented in pitiful voice:

"'Alas, beloved son, delightful, handsome, why have you come too quickly under the power of death? Why did death not come first to me? There will be for me no other woe greater than this.'

"And the queen, having regained her senses, with dishevelled hair, beating her breast with her arms, writhing on the ground like a fish thrown up onto dry land, like a female buffalo who has lost her young, like a she-camel who has lost her offspring, wailed in a pitiful voice:

"'Alas, beloved son, by whom has this lotus **(223)** been broken and scattered over the ground? Who is my enemy on the earth, who has now slain my son, whose eyes were captivating the heart, whose face resembled the moon? Alas, why does not this body now perish, since I behold my excellent son slain upon the ground? Quite clearly this heart of mine is made of iron, since having perceived such disaster it has not broken. Alas, this fruit has resulted from that evil dream when today in the midst of my dream someone cut off my two breasts with a sword and wrenched out my teeth: today my beloved son has swiftly perished. **(224)** Just as one of the three doves I held here was snatched away by a falcon, today, when surrounded by my three sons, one has been taken away by death.'

"Then the king and the queen made laments of many kinds in pitiful voice. Taking off all their ornaments, they paid homage to the relics of their son in the company of a large crowd and deposited the prince's relics in this place.

"If indeed, Ānanda, you should think that he was another, he was at that time, at that moment, the royal prince called Mahāsattva. Yet it is not to be viewed thus. Why is that? At that time, at that moment, *I* was the royal prince called Mahāsattva. Even then, Ānanda, when I was not wholly free from passion, hatred, and folly, I helped the whole world with their woes such as hells. How much more would I now, when I am free of every defect and have attained perfect enlightenment, endure[(189)] in the hells an aeon for the sake of every single being or deliver them from the cycle of birth? **(225)** I, the best of beings, have helped the whole world with numerous different very difficult acts."

Then the Lord at that time uttered these verses:

"During many aeons I have sacrificed myself while seeking this supreme enlightenment. Just as I became king or prince, so I sacrificed my body. I remember in former births there was a king called Mahāratha. And he had a very generous son called the excellent Mahāsattva. And then he had two brothers called Mahādeva and Mahāpraṇāda. And the brothers went together into a wild forest. **(226)** They saw a tigress overcome by hunger. Compassion arose in that excellent being: 'Wherefore now I will sacrifice myself, for this tigress, oppressed by hunger and thirst, will devour her own offspring.' And Mahāsattva, the son of Mahāratha, fell down the mountain-side, when he saw the hungry tigress, in order to save the cubs of the tigress, out of compassion. The earth with its mountains shook. Various flocks of birds flew off. A herd of deer was terrified. This world was filled with darkness. His two brothers, Mahāpraṇāda and Mahādeva, having looked in that great, excellent forest, did not find Mahāsattva. **(227)** With extreme grief and pain in their hearts,[(190)] they wandered about, senseless, in the forest. They searched for their brother, their faces (covered) with tears. They wandered about in the middle of the forest. Both those princes, Mahāpraṇāda and Mahādeva, went to where the weak tigress lay. Seeing the tigress and her cubs,

[(189)] Read *samutsaheyaṃ* with MS. G (Skjærvø).

[(190)] Read *-hṛdayā* (misprint).

the lips of the tigress smeared with blood, and seeing some hairs and bones scattered and fallen on the ground, since a few drops of his blood had fallen on the ground, the two princes beheld the blood-sprinkled ground. Made faint and with their minds impaired, they fell there upon the ground, their limbs smeared with mud and dust, bereft of their sense of memory, with confused thoughts. And their attendants, lamenting in pitiful voice, oppressed with grief, besprinkled them with water and wept standing with arms upraised. (**228**) And as soon as he had fallen, his mother and bearer, the beloved chief queen, together with five hundred women, went inside the palace and sat down in comfort. Produced from both the nipples on her breasts, milk suddenly flowed for all her body was tormented as if being pricked by needles. Her heart full of extreme grief, pierced by the arrow of the extreme grief of the loss of her son, she approached the king with very sorrowful mind, consumed by grief, weeping in pitiful voice, and then she said to King Mahāratha: 'Listen to me, king, lord of men. My body burns with the fire of grief. (**229**) From both the nipples on my breasts milk has suddenly been produced. My body is tormented as if being pricked by needles. And my heart is bursting. Since the sign was such, I will not again behold the sight of my beloved sons. In my separation from my sons, give me my life. Have compassion. In a dream today I saw my three young doves. The third young dove is beloved and attractive to me. A falcon entered there, and the young dove was snatched away by the falcon. (**230**) In my dream such grief entered this heart of mine. As a result of thinking[(191)] too much on the fire of my grief, there will ere long be death for me. In my separation from my sons, give me my life. Let there be compassion.' Having spoken thus, the chief queen fainted and fell upon the ground there, for she was bereft of her sense of memory, her thoughts failed, and her mind was unconscious. And the whole crowd in the harem wept and wailed in pitiful voice on seeing the chief queen fallen unconscious there upon the ground. Immediately, the king, afflicted with the grief of losing his son, went with his ministers and attendants to find out about the princes. The people in the whole city came out of their various houses and stood

[(191)] Read *-cittān* Nobel, Nachtrag.

(there). Thus did they come. (**231**) Their faces (covered) with tears, weeping, they inquired after Mahāsattva on the roads: 'Is he alive or dead? Where now has Mahāsattva gone? Will I see today him who is charming, who is beloved and charming to the sight of beings?' Suddenly the wind of grief, which cannot be heard, went forth in this region, fierce, without making a noise, (yet) with a sharp sound due to limitless magic.[(192)] King Mahāratha rose up, weeping, afflicted with grief, and besprinkled his chief queen, who had fallen on the ground, with streams of water. He besprinkled her with water until she regained her memory. And she rose up and, with unhappy mind, she asked: 'Have my sons died or do they live?' And King Mahāratha spoke thus to his chief queen: (**232**) 'The ministers and attendants have gone in the subdirections to find out about the princes. Do not be too unhappy in mind (or) continually with grief in your heart.' And thus did Mahāratha console his chief queen. He went out of the royal palace with his face (covered) with tears, weeping, sick with grief, attended by a group of ministers, with very unhappy mind and with unhappy eyes. Going out of the excellent city to find out about the princes, many hundreds of thousands of beings, with their faces (covered) with tears, weeping, ran off. Seeing that the king had gone out, they joined up behind the king. King Mahāratha departed from the city immediately. (**233**) With rolling eyes he looked[(193)] in the (ten) directions to see his beloved son. He saw coming (towards him) a certain man, whose head had been shaved, whose limbs were smeared with blood, whose body was smeared with mud, his face (covered) with tears, weeping. And fierce grief arose in the heart of King Mahāratha. With his face (covered) with tears, he wept, and standing with arms upraised, he lamented. Then a certain minister came hurriedly, quickly, from afar. He approached the lord of men and spoke to King Mahāratha: 'Do not have grief in your mind, king. Your charming

[(192)] The text is obscure. My translation is based on the reading *ananta-māyā-sa-kaṭu-nirghoṣaḥ*. All MSS have *ananta-māyā*, which Nobel emended to *ananta-māyāḥ*. *nirghoṣaḥ*, the reading of MS. G is to be preferred to *nighoṣaḥ*. The choice of *nirghoṣa* here may have been deliberate since it means both 'sound' and 'soundless'.

[(193)] Reading *prekṣati*. See Nobel, Sanskrit text, p.233 n.2.

sons are alive. (**234**) Soon you will see your excellent delightful son coming here into your presence.' The king went on for just a moment.[194] Then there came a second minister. Covered with dust and clad in filthy garments, with his face (bathed) in tears, he said this to the king: 'Two of your sons, great king, are alive (but) blazing with the fire of grief. One excellent son of yours is not visible, king. Mahāsattva was consumed by impermanence, and when he saw the tigress, who had recently given birth, desirous of eating her very own cubs, the excellent prince Mahāsattva produced a great power[195] of compassion for them and made a noble resolve for enlightenment: "And I will deliver all the beings here. May I in future time attain the profound, noble enlightenment, which I have desired." (**235**) Then Mahāsattva fell down the mountain-side. The tigress arose, overcome with hunger. In a moment she made his body without flesh and left the prince with only some bones remaining.' And having heard thus the very dreadful speech, King Mahāratha fainted. And he fell upon the ground, his thoughts having failed. And the fire of his grief blazed very fiercely. (**236**) His ministers and attendants, weeping in pitiful voice, afflicted with grief, besprinkled him with water. Standing with upraised arms and lamenting, a third minister said to the king: 'I have today seen both princes in a faint there in that great forest. They both fell upon the ground, their thoughts having failed, and we besprinkled them with water, until they regained their memory. Ablaze, they looked in the four directions. For a moment they stood, (then) they fell to the ground (and) wailed with a pitiful voice. Those two continually stood with upraised arms and uttered praise of this brother.' And the king had sad thoughts in his heart. (**237**) His thoughts were distraught because of the loss of his son. Burning with grief he lamented, for thus the king was reflecting[196]: 'One of my sons, beloved, delightful, has been devoured by the great Rākṣasa of impermanence. May these my other two sons not attain the destruction of their life through the fire of their grief. Wherefore now I will quickly proceed there. I will behold those two sons of beloved

[194] Read °*mātram* with MSS. ABCDEF.

[195] Better would be *°cittaṃ* 'thought'. See Nobel, Sanskrit text, p.234 n.27.

[196] Reading *paricintayantaḥ*. See Nobel, Sanskrit text, p.237 n.3.

appearance. And I (will bring them) by a speedy vehicle to the capital and make them enter the royal palace speedily. (**238**) May the heart of their mother and bearer not burst on account of the fire of her grief. And seeing her two sons, may she obtain peace and not find loss of life.' And the king, together with a group of ministers, mounted his elephant and went to see his sons. And seeing his two sons crossing the path together,[(197)] he lamented their brother's name in a pitiful voice. The king took his two sons, and weeping, proceeded to the city. Very quickly, like one in a hurry, he showed the queen her own two sons."

"And I, the Tathāgata Śākyamuni, was formerly the excellent Mahāsattva, (**239**) the son of King Mahāratha, by whom the tigress was made happy. For Śuddhodana, the excellent king, was King Mahāratha by name. And the excellent Queen Māyā was the chief queen. Likewise, Maitreya was Mahāpraṇāda. Then there was the king's son Mahādeva: he was Mañjuśrī the Prince. Mahāprajāpatī was the tigress there. The five monks were the cubs of the tigress."

"Then the great king and the great queen made many different pitiful lamentations, took off all their ornaments, and together with a large crowd they did homage to the relics of their son. (**240**) They deposited those relics of Mahāsattva in that place and built this stūpa made of the seven jewels. And when Mahāsattva gave up his body to the tigress, he made the following resolve through compassion: 'Through this sacrifice of my body may all beings in future time during aeons exceeding calculation be caused to perform the Buddha-act.'

While this exposition was being expounded, innumerable beings, creatures including men and gods, raised their thought to supreme and perfect enlightenment. And this is the reason, this the cause of the revelation of this stūpa here. And that stūpa, through the Buddha's blessing, entered the ground at that very spot.

So (ends) the eighteenth chapter, the Chapter on the Tigress, in the excellent Suvarṇabhāsa, king of sūtras. (**241**)

[(197)] This rendering is based on the reading *saṃtarāṇa mārga* proposed by Skjærvø on account of manuscript J *satarā mārgni* and G *satarā (mārga?)*.

19. CHAPTER ON THE PRAISE OF ALL THE TATHĀGATAS

Then indeed those numerous hundreds of thousands of Bodhisattvas approached the Tathāgata Suvarṇaratnākaracchatrakūṭa. Having approached, they worshipped with their head the feet of Suvarṇaratnākaracchatrakūṭa and stood on one side. Having stood on one side, the numerous hundreds of thousands of Bodhisattvas placed their hands in the gesture of reverence and praised the Tathāgata Suvarṇaratnākaracchatrakūṭa in the following verses:

"The Buddha's body is like the colour of gold. His members are brilliant with the colour of gold. He has the colour of gold like the golden lord of mountains. The seer is a white lotus of golden colour. His members are adorned with major marks that are good. His members are decorated with various good minor marks. He is very brilliant, with the fine splendour of gold. He is very pure, placid, like the lord of mountains. He has the Brahma-voice, the sound of pleasant-voiced Brahma. He has the lion's voice, the sound of a thundering cloud. His sixtyfold thundering voice is a very pure voice. **(242)** The Buddha's voice has the sound of a peacock or an Indian cuckoo. The Buddha is very pure, very brilliant with very flawless splendour, fully adorned with the marks of hundreds of merits. The Buddha is an ocean of very pure, very flawless knowledge, is endowed with all the fine virtues of Sumeru. The Buddha has supreme compassion for the welfare of beings, is an excellent giver of blessing in the worlds, a good expositor of the highest truth, a leader to the blessing of complete Nirvāṇa. He is a giver of the blessing of nectar. [(198) The Buddha is an excellent expositor of the nectar of the Law, a leader to the city of nectar, a mine of all blessings, a place of blessing. The Buddha delivers beings from woe, releases creatures from the ocean of woe, leads creatures excellently on the path of peace and gives every blessing to creatures. It is impossible in your case to make comparison with the extent of the ocean of virtue and knowledge of the Buddha. You have compassion for all beings,] the power of love, expedients, and heroism.(199) It is not possible in the midst of the world

(198) Translated from the Tibetan. The Sanskrit is missing.

(199) Reading *°vīryavantaṃ* with MSS. ABCDE.

of the gods to expound in many thousands of millions of aeons one by one the merits from a drop out of the ocean of your virtue and knowledge. (**243**) This has been expounded briefly by me. What is (it but) a drop of virtue arising from an ocean of virtue? And whatever heap of merit I have heaped up, through that may beings touch supreme enlightenment."

Then indeed the Bodhisattva Ruciraketu rose from his seat, covered one shoulder with his upper garment, placed his right knee on the ground, put his hands in the gesture of reverence towards the Lord and at that time praised the Lord in the following verses:

"Lord of sages, you have the marks of hundreds of merits and are adorned with thousands of splendid, brilliant virtues. You have a noble complexion, an excellent, placid appearance, a brightness issued as it were by a thousand suns. Your brightness is filled with the burning of numerous rays. (**244**) You resemble jewels full of various colours. You have the brilliance of blue, white or gold, the brilliance of beryl, coppery dawn or crystal. You illuminate Sumeru-mountains. You light up numerous millions of fields. You becalm the fierce, severe woes. You satisfy beings with excellent blessings. Your complexion and senses are pure and you are beautiful to behold. Your beauty causes insatiableness. You are pleasing for people to behold. The hair on your head shines with the colour of a peacock. Its splendour is like a lotus full of bees. (**245**) You are adorned with the pure virtues of compassion. You have accumulated excellent merits by meditation and love. You are equipped with minor marks in various colours. You are adorned with (such) virtues as the (seven) members of enlightenment (including) meditations.[200] For you are a bringer of joy, a bringer of good, a bringer of blessing, the source of a mine of every blessing. You are adorned with various profound virtues. You shine in thousands of millions of fields. You blaze with beams, which as it were cause fire, and you are like the sun's full orb

[200] The seven 'members of enlightenment' (*bodhyaṅga*) are said to be: *smṛti* 'mindfulness', *dharmapravicaya* 'study of the Law', *vīrya* 'fortitude', *prīti* 'joy', *prasrabdhi* 'serenity', *samādhi* 'meditation', and *upekṣā* 'equanimity'. For further details see *Encyclopaedia of Buddhism*, ed. G.P. Malalasekera, s.v. *bojjhaṅga*.

in the sky. Endowed with all virtues like Sumeru, (**246**) you[(201)] appear in all the world-spheres. Resembling cow-milk, a conch, a white lily or the moon, having the colour of snow, like a beautiful white lotus, the row of your teeth shines out from your face just as the sky is as it were (brightened) by royal geese. The hair-circle in the middle of your placid face, your moon-like countenance, turns to the right, is very curly, beryl-coloured, black. With its rays it shines like the sun in the sky." (**247**)

Then indeed the noble goddess Bodhisattvasamuccayā at that time praised the Lord in the following verses:

"Homage be to the Buddha, whose enlightenment is pure, who has realized eloquence in the pure Law, who has realized a self free from the paths of lawlessness, who has a pure realization of the knowledge of existence and non-existence. How endless is the Buddha's glory! How he resembles the ocean or Meru! How endless is the Buddha's sphere, difficult to obtain as is the flower of the *uḍumbara*-tree![(202)] How compassionate is the Tathāgata, a banner in the family of Śākya kings, a sun among the lords of men, since he has spoken such an excellent sūtra for the aid of all beings! (**248**) With his senses calm, the Tathāgata Śākyamuni, calm, excellent, entered the calm city. Profound, calm, flawless was his meditation. He entered that sphere of the victorious Buddha."

"And the bodies of the Śrāvakas are empty. The dwelling-places of the best of the two-footed are empty. All those things and their nature are empty. And beings are empty. A self is not found at all."

"Constantly, constantly, I recollect the Buddha. And constantly I am anxious for sight of the Buddha. And always, constantly, I make

(201) Reading *saṃdṛśyase* with MSS. ABCDEF.

(202) The reference is to the rarity of Buddhas. More explicit is Mahāvastu (ed. E. Senart) i.233-234:

> *udumbarasya yatha puṣpaṃ dullabhaṃ*
> *kadācid utpadyati loke māṇava*
> *evam eva buddhāna mahāyaśāna*
> *kadācid utpādaṃ tathāgatānāṃ*

"As the blossom of the glomerous fig-tree but rarely is found appearing in the world, O young brāhman, so is it with the appearance of glorious Buddhas and Tathāgatas" (tr. J.J. Jones, i.190).

a resolve in order to see the Buddha-sun. Constantly standing with my knee on the ground, I am consumed with exceeding anxiety to see the Buddha. (**249**) Weeping pitifully for the sake of the Buddha, I am extremely desirous of seeing him who has attained bliss. I am constantly ablaze with the fire of anxiety. Give me the cool water of his appearance. I am extremely desirous of seeing your form. Gladden me with the water of compassion. Act for me with the feeling of compassion, Buddha. Grant me your appearance, your placid form. For the world with its gods has been protected by you. And thus are the bodies of the Śrāvakas empty. (**250**) And all beings are by nature a dream, equal to space, having the sky as their nature, resembling magic, a mirage, the moon (reflected) in water. Empty are the great ones of you, the Buddha. [The sphere of the Tathāgata is pure like crystal. You enter the city of the supreme nectar of the Law. You are able to bring to beings unlimited blessings. The sphere of the Tathāgata is subtle, wonderful, and very profound. Among all beings none is able to know it. Among seers possessed of the five kinds of supernatural knowledge, among all the Śrāvakas and all the Pratyekabuddhas, none is able to know it. Now I have no doubt concerning the sphere of the Buddha. May you therefore out of mercy and compassion show me your body!][(203)]"

Then the Lord rose up from his seat and spoke with the Brahma-voice: "Bravo, bravo to you, noble goddess! Bravo to you, noble goddess, and again bravo!"

This the Lord said, and the Bodhisattvas headed by the noble goddess Bodhisattvasamuccayā and the great goddess Sarasvatī, and the whole assembly, (**251**) headed by gods, men, Asuras, Garuḍas, Kiṃnaras, Mahoragas and the like, joyfully acclaimed the Lord's speech.

The noble, excellent Suvarṇabhāsa, king of sūtras, is finished.

[(203)] Verses 30–31 are not extant in Sanskrit or Tib. I but are partially preserved in Khotanese (N. p.90), as recognized by Nobel. He also noted that the Khotanese version agrees substantially with that of Dharmakṣema. The translation given here is accordingly based on Dharmakṣema.

INDEX OF PROPER NAMES

References are to the text, page, and line of Nobel

APPENDIX: THE KHOTANESE INTRODUCTION

The improved translation of the Khotanese introduction here appended owes much to the research of Professor P.O. Skjærvø. For detailed commentary the reader must await the publication of his critical edition.

... This (is) my petition to the Lord Buddhas and to the Bodhisattvas and to gods, goddesses, men, Nāgas, (and) Yakṣas. May they receive this my worship of the Law, (this) auspicious prayer ...

These are the reasons provided by it in this sūtra on account of which it is called the 'King of Sūtras'.

The career of the Buddhas is expounded by it, and by it the very noble (doctrine of) emptiness (is expounded) in a good way, and the body of the Law of the Lord Buddhas is expounded by it, and the manifestation of the life (of the Tathāgatas is expounded by it to be) unlimited, and the very difficult former acts (of the Buddhas) and the *meditations (are expounded) by it, (and also) the very difficult acts of the Bodhisattva, and the prophecies of many divine sons (to enlightenment), and eulogies (are expounded) by it, and confessions, and ripenings and congratulations, and entreaties, and supplications, and the great Buddha-power, and the destruction of evil acts (are expounded by it), and *dhāraṇīs*. And here in this sūtra the caring for all beings in this birth (and) in other births is expounded. And the knowledge of kings is expounded by it, how it sustains the beings of (the king's) land, how they (the kings) establish them (the beings) in the Law so that they do not at all go to an evil state, how they can be cared for with the things of this birth: this (is) the exposition in this sūtra. How too one removes the bodily diseases of diseased beings, this exposition (is found) here. Therefore is this sūtra called 'King of Sūtras.' Of the holders of all other sūtras too (it is) the supporter. Therefore is this (sūtra) called the 'King of Sūtras.' 'Suvarṇa' means 'gold'; 'bhāsa' means 'shining'. Just as among precious substances gold, it has been said, shines best, so this sūtra for such reasons as these shines best. Therefore is it called the 'Suvarṇabhāsottama', because (it is) the best (sūtra).

Since I have ordered this Suvarṇabhāsottama Sūtra to be written in Khotanese and (thus) made it understandable ... whatever good there may have accrued to me here, I share it with all my relatives, beginning with my mother, father, sisters, (and) brother, with (my) friends, spiritual advisers, (and) all *kinsmen. And with the whole land of Khotan, and with all the beings in the land of Khotan I share (it). And in that manner I share with all beings this good. And may I thereby surely obtain unrestricted enlightenment. And this good too and these merits I take to the Four Great Kings, and to the Great Goddess Śrī–to them (goes) the very best share among these merits of mine here. May that (share) surely so prosper through the merits of the Buddhas (and) the Bodhisattvas as it has been expounded in this sūtra.